C2

2

Ayli Valley

Young ranch hand Owen Lismore is on the run from his brother and the notorious gunman Josh Bassinet. The law also wants to question him and his one regret is having to leave the lovely Rosalind behind. However, while hiding out with a rustler band in the Arden Mountains, he rescues Rosalind and her friends from a colony of hillbillies.

But when Bassinet kills Owen's brother and best friend, he knows he can never rest easy or return home to claim the family ranch while the gunman still lives. Everyone warns him he doesn't stand a chance against the killer.

With these dire warnings ringing in his ears, Owen rides in for the showdown.

Ayli Valley

Gary Astill

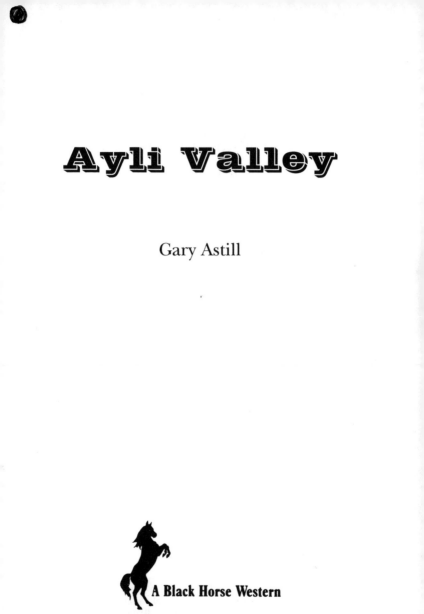

A Black Horse Western

ROBERT HALE · LONDON

ISBN-10: 0-7090-8162-6
ISBN-13: 978-0-7090-8162-3

Robert Hale Limited
Clerkenwell House
Clerkenwell Green
London EC1R 0HT

To Hillary Ashton
My help in ages past

Typeset by
Derek Doyle & Associates, Shaw Heath
Printed and bound in Great Britain by
Antony Rowe Limited, Wiltshire

1

The youngster's face was flushed from his exertions and sweat poured down his lean cheeks. He was crouched in a fighting stance with his fists balled. Beneath his cotton shirt knotted muscles bulged and writhed as he worked his arms, feinting and ducking. Moving lightly on his feet he looked for an opening.

The man facing him couldn't have been more different. For a start he was large and heavily built. A slight smile played about his lips as he swayed and moved before the youngster. His nose had been flattened in some earlier bout and gave his face a battered look – like an old bull that had been buffeted in many bruising affrays.

'Come on boy. Can't you hit dis ol' Swede fella. Maybe you want a bigga target.' The man spoke with a slight foreign accent. Suddenly he chuckled. 'Aren't I big enough for you to hit?'

His smile broadened as the young boy lunged forward with a flurry of punches. The big man back-pedalled and swayed from side to side in an effort to avoid the blows. Some of the punches landed but most missed their intended mark.

For a big man he could move fast. However his movements were fluid and effortless. His own hand flipped out and he batted the young man on the side of the head. The boy swung wildly in a futile effort to land a telling blow on his opponent. He was cuffed a few more times before he danced back out of range. He was breathing heavily from his exertions.

'Damn you, Adam, you devil! The only way I'm gonna hit you is if I sneak up behind you with an axe-handle and clobber you while you're asleep.'

The big man dropped his arms and grinned broadly. 'Even den I still get up and push axe up your lazy ass.'

The boy wiped sweat from his brow. 'Can't we have a break now? I think I'd as soon rope a herd of steers as have these here boxing lessons from you.'

'Dat reminds me, Master Owen, if your brudder come back and find we not finish dat dere branding we in heap pile of trouble.'

'Damn my brother! I have to do all the work round here while he goes off gambling and sparking the ladies in town. It ain't goddamn right!'

'You shouldn't swear dat much, Master Owen. How you join polite society if you use dat kinda language?'

'I hate my brother.'

'Hate is strong word, Master Owen. Remember the Old Testament story of Cain and Abel. Cain hated his brudder and it made him to murder Abel.'

'Well if Abel was anything like Oliver, I can't say I blame Cain.'

Shaking his head the older man walked to the water-trough and bending low, dunked his head in the water. He came up spraying water and snorting like a wild bull. The youngster stepped beside him and performed the same cooling-off exercise.

'Tell me true, Adam, am I ever going to be good enough to take on John Charles in the competition next week?'

'You is coming on fine, Master Owen. You be ready well

in time. You got youth, stamina and strength. Jus'you listen to ol' Adam here. You got to box. Don't mix it. Charles knows a lot of dirty tricks when he get you close. He really hurt you if you let him get you in the clinch. The footwork I teach you is what win you the bout.' Reaching out he affectionately rubbed the back of the youth's head with a big meaty hand. 'Why you want fight beats me. You have comfortable life here. Your brudder not bad fella. When you of age he give you share of ranch.'

'Goddamn it, Adam,' the youngster interrupted fiercely. 'I fight for the five hundred dollars in prize money. Oliver keeps me starved of cash. He says the ranch ain't doing any good and he has to plough all the money back in the ranch. Last month he sold those steers in Abilene. He musta got two or three thousand for that deal. I never saw a dime of that. My guess is he spends it on women and gambling in town. Damn his rotten, stinking soul!'

'Master Owen, I not have you swearing. It . . . it . . . not dignified.'

Owen grinned widely at his mentor. 'If'n you weren't so doggone good at fisticuffs I'd whip your starchy ass for that sass.'

The big hands reached for the youth but he danced out of reach, leaving the older man shaking his head in mock exasperation. Before any more horseplay could take place both men stopped and listened to the sound of hoofbeats approaching the ranch buildings.

'Boy, dat be your brudder, I bet. He back early an' he not be pleased we not finish dat branding.'

A big, mottled gelding pounded into the yard. At the last minute the rider hauled on the rains and the horse shuddered to a halt in front of the barn. Its flanks were heaving and froth speckled its jaws. The rider was laughing and turned to watch as another horse and rider

7

followed him into the yard.

'Yippeee!' The first rider yelled. 'That's twenty dollars you owe me, Josh.'

The second rider was a lean, dark-haired man with deep-set eyes and a close-cropped, black beard. He was dressed from head to toe in black leather. As he dismounted a pair of low-slung matching black Colts could be seen belted around his waist.

'I guess you're right, Oliver. You sure ride like the devil's up your ass.'

Oliver threw back his head and laughed aloud. He was a very handsome young man in his mid twenties. He was wearing an expensive tailor-made shirt with a silk kerchief knotted round his neck. With a smooth movement he slid from his panting mount. Without looking at the man he ordered Adam to take care of his horse, then walked towards the house. Suddenly he noticed his younger brother standing near the barn glowering at him. He swung round.

'You look like you ate something sour, brother,' he observed. 'You finished that branding?'

Instead of answering Owen ignored his brother and stared with some curiosity at his brother's black-garbed companion.

'I heard you call this fella Josh. Is he who I think he is – Josh Bassinet?'

The man he was enquiring about was standing beside his mount. He returned the youngster's stare without any hint of warmth.

'Brother, I asked you a question,' Oliver demanded. 'I'm still awaiting an answer.'

'And I asked you, is this the killer, Josh Bassinet?'

'You insolent puppy!'

With a few quick steps Oliver was by his brother's side. He was still carrying his riding quirt and with a swift movement he raised it and slashed it across his brother's shoulder. The reaction was swift and purely instinctive. Owen's clenched fist hit his brother in the abdomen and as the elder brother gasped and bent over the other fist came up with a neat uppercut to the chin. Oliver slammed against the barn door and bounced back to be met with a right cross. He hit the ground and lay in the dust of the yard, blood seeping from his nose. Owen stood over his brother with clenched fists, his young face tight with anger.

'Get up, Oliver! Get on your feet. I'm gonna thrash you. That's the last time you hit me. You hear me?'

Oliver lay on his back staring up at his brother. He wiped a hand across his mouth. Blood smeared his lips.

'I'll kill you for this, Owen. You're finished here. Get off this ranch. I never want to see you again.

'OK, Oliver if that's what you want. But I want my share of the ranch. Pa left the ranch to me as well as you. I was to get my share as soon as I came of age. You pay me my share and I'll go. I won't go empty-handed.'

'You'll do as your brother says. You'll pack your things and get lost.'

The black-clad gunman moved close to the brothers. His eyes were cold as he stared at the angry youngster. The gloved hands hovered near his gun butts – the threat of gunplay implicit in his stance and attitude. Owen stared in defiance at this gunman.

'You're a brave man facing an unarmed youngster, fella.'

The voice came from behind. The gunman went very still. In a blur of movement he whirled and the guns were in his hands. That was as far as he got. A big clenched fist hit him on the side of the head. As he staggered back another fist hit him in the face and another. His boots snagged against the fallen Oliver and he sprawled to the ground. With swift movements Adam recovered the Colts

9

from the dazed gunman. His look was contemptuous as he turned and tossed the weapons into the water-trough.

'Come, Master Owen, dat branding won't get done wit all dis here fooling.'

Owen's eyes were round with excitement and wonder as he stared at his big companion. 'You know who that is? That's Josh Bassinet the gunfighter!'

Adam turned and walked away. Owen had no option but to trail behind his companion. They left behind two bitter men. Men who had ridden into the yard so full of self-importance – now lying in the dirt of the yard, battered and very angry at the rough treatment received at the hands of a couple of common ranch hands.

2

'That Swede is dead.' The voice was full of venom. 'What about that brother of yours? You want I should take care of him at the same time?'

The two men had clambered to their feet. Oliver looked down with some distaste at the dirt on his clothes. He made ineffectual efforts to dust himself down. Josh Bassinet had walked over to the water-trough and with sleeves rolled up was fishing out his pistols. Using the trigger guard he hung each one on the wooden edge. He swore viciously and colourfully as he regarded the tools of his trade, now sopping wet.

'Damn Swede is above his station. Why the hell you allow him to stay on here beats me.'

'He worked for my father. He found him at a boxing-booth. The owners were using him to fight anyone as cared to challenge him. The old fool offered him a job here and he's stayed ever since.' Oliver stared balefully after the two cowboys. 'Just leave him alone for the time being. I want rid of my brother but in such a way that won't connect me to the deed. Once I've solved that problem then the Swede's yours.'

The gunman shot a venomous look at the rancher. 'Just you say the word and I'll take care of them both. No one hits Josh Bassinet and lives to boast of it.'

'Just lay off for now. I'll tell you when.'

'I'll have to dismantle these guns and clean them. I can't risk them misfiring after that dousing. Goddamn that Swede to hell!'

'Come up the house. We can have a drink while I think this out.'

Down in the corral the boxers had returned to the branding. The fire they had left piled high with logs was now a bright-red glow of embers. Adam stood by the fire, his hand on a wooden-handled branding-iron. He watched as Owen came running a steer and expertly wrestled the bawling animal to the ground beside the fire. The beast struggled wildly. Owen lay across the forelegs, his arms and shoulders straining to keep the battling animal in position. Swiftly the Swede jabbed the branding-iron onto the side of the steer. The smell of singed hair and toasted flesh stung the nostrils. The beast protested loudly.

Owen rolled away from the steer. Bawling indignantly it gained its feet and kicking out its hind legs in a futile effort to disable its tormentor fled to the safety of the herd. Even as the beast was released the youngster was on his feet and racing to select another animal. Adam pushed the iron into the embers again and waited for the next offering. It was this physical wrestling with his charges that had given Owen his strength of arm and shoulder.

The longhorn was no demure domestic animal. It was half-wild from living and foraging out on the range. Every beast had to be driven and chivvied by the men who worked the herds. It was an unremitting struggle with recalcitrant steers and Owen loved the work and the sheer physical challenge of the labour.

Back on his pony Owen quickly cut out another beast and drove it towards his partner. His rope snaked out and dropped neatly onto the steer. The cowpony was almost as adept as was the cowpuncher, knowing just when to change direction and tighten the rope the rider had twined around the pommel. The steer went down and Owen, leaping nimbly from his pony, gripped the horns. Adam was there with the hot iron and another beast was branded with the letters AYLI.

Owen's father Alex Lismore had started the ranch by doing what his son was now doing. He had caught and branded wild steers. His wife Yvette had come up with the brand design made up of the initials of their names. The basin they worked became known as Ayli Valley.

Alex Lismore had owned the biggest ranch in the area. That changed with the arrival in the area of Leonard Duke. Now, after only a few short years since that advent Alex Lismore was dead. Killed in a riding accident was the official version. Muttered in private was the suspicion that an expert horseman like Alex Lismore was most unlikely to have had an accident with his mount.

For Leonard Duke, the demise of the man who stood in the way of his acquisitions was opportune. He was in a position to cajole and bully Lismore's heir, the flamboyant and extravagant Oliver Lismore, into parting with large swaths of his inherited land. With grazing for his own herds secured Leonard Duke had set out to gobble up the small ranchers in Ayli Valley. Those unwilling to sell out to the newcomer found that disaster and even death resulted. Leonard Duke's empire grew and prospered.

Up in the ranch house Oliver, looking surly and mean, was nursing a glass of whiskey along with his injured pride. Nearby sat Josh Bassinet, busy cleaning his weapons.

'I tell you, I should have shot that upstart Swede,' the gunman muttered savagely. 'Nobody, but nobody treats me like that. We let him away with this and you won't never have no peace.'

13

'I'm thinking, Josh, I'm thinking. I can't have my brother's blood on my hands. If that happened I'd never be able to live in this community. People thought it funny my old man died in that accident. There was a lot of talk at the time. But no one actually pointed the finger at me. If Owen were to meet with the same fate I'd never live that down. It would reopen all the old rumours about my father's death.'

'That Swede's been teaching him to box. That's why he was able to down you. I tell you, let me kill the Swede and that'll solve half your problem.'

Oliver was staring at his friend, a sudden light in his eye.

'Boxing! You got it Josh. He's put his name down for the boxing show coming to town.'

Josh looked up from his cleaning. 'What good's that? No one's never died from no boxing, at least not as far as I know.'

'John Charles – he did kill a man once over in Kentucky. Was a lot of bad publicity over it. That's why he's had to take this job with a travelling show. They claim they'll pay five hundred dollars to anyone as will stay three rounds with him. That's what Owen is after. He wants that five hundred.'

'So?'

'So we get to Charles and offer him an incentive to make sure my brother don't leave the ring alive.'

There was a sudden light in Josh's eyes as he looked at his friend.

'Son of a bitch! If that ain't the sweetest deal I ever did hear. With your brother safely out of the way I pick a fight with that there Swede and we solve our problem. Son of a bitch.'

The men grinned at each other and raised their glasses.

14

3

'Consarn it, you ox, I asked for my rig to be ready at two.'

Celia Duke was petite and dainty and fiery. What she lacked in size she made up for in petulance.

The groom was red-faced and panting as he struggled with the harness. He was a young man, broad in the shoulder with a larger than average head and hands like frying-pans. The pony he was working with was almost the equine version of its mistress. The ears were drawn back flat on its skull as it eyed the hapless youth.

'I do my best, Miss Celia,' he panted. 'The job ain't made any easier with this she-cat of a pony.'

The head came round and there was the audible snap of teeth. Fortunately for the groom he read the signs correctly and withdrew his hand just in time.

'Henry, your job is to work with horses. If you can't manage I'm sure Father can find someone who can.'

The voice of the girl had gone mild and sweet. Somehow it was the more threatening for all that. Henry cast a sideways look at the girl. She had turned her back on him and was staring out through the stable doors, irritably slapping her riding-whip against her leg. Henry shouldn't have taken his attention off the pony.

'Aaahh!'

Henry staggered back from the harness, rubbing furiously at his arm. His sleeve was ripped and as he rubbed a red tinge of blood seeped onto his fingers.

'Son of a bitch! I'm gonna take a axe-handle to that there brute and teach her a lesson.'

'For God's sake, you stupid boy! Can't you do anything without making such a fuss? I might just as well harness up Moth myself.'

Celia brushed the youth aside – he and she were of a similar age but she was dwarfed by his size. She looked like a child beside his bulk. Expertly, she finished buckling on the harness. The pony stood docile while the girl worked.

'It's you – you stupid boy! You agitate poor Moth. You're so bloody dumb.' Her task finished, she turned and glared at the distraught youth. 'There!' She indicated the harness, now buckled into position. 'Was that so hard?'

He made no answer – just shuffled his feet, not looking at her.

'Now, would it be beyond your capabilities to lead her out into the yard? I would like to have my outing today.'

Minutes later Celia was driving the buggy out of town. She was smirking as she relished the humiliation of her father's groom. She flicked the reins.

'Come along, you naughty little madam,' she called to the pony. 'Have you no respect for the dumb brutes of this world?'

The place Celia was seeking was a large run-down house at the mouth of Ayli Valley. It was situated on the side of a hill and overlooked the trail that led out into the mountainous region of Arden. The young woman who waited for Celia outside the house was tall, with long, auburn hair hanging down her back. She leaned her rifle against a fence post and waved a greeting. When Celia pulled up in front of the house she scowled at her friend.

'Why can't you live in town like a civilized person? Any time I want to see you I have to drag all the way out here.'

16

The tall girl laughed. 'I see you're in a good mood today, Celia.'

Celia climbed down, muttering and grumbling. Her friend wrapped her arms around her. As Celia struggled to escape the embrace some of the ill-humour eased from her expression.

'For goodness sake, Rosalind, will you stop mauling me. You're like a great bear slobbering over me.'

Rosalind laughed out loud. 'Oh, I do love you, Celia. You are a bad-tempered dwarf but you are also my best friend. Come.' She released her friend and retrieved her rifle. 'Come up the house for a glass of lemonade.'

'Hang on. I brought you some stuff.' Celia pulled a bulging sack from the cart. She heaved the heavy bag towards Rosalind. 'You carry it. Not only do you look like a grizzly bear but you are as strong as one.'

Later they sat companionably on the porch and drank lemonade. The view was quite stunning looking across the width of the valley. The far slopes were covered with piñon and juniper trees. Out of lush, steep-sided canyons, cataracts erupted and flushed down the slopes to empty into the rapid-flowing Estelle River.

'I've told you before, Celia, I don't need charity. It was good of you to bring me that sack of groceries but I manage quite well out here by myself.'

'It's not charity, you great lummox, it's a gift from a friend.'

Rosalind eyed the smaller girl fondly but said nothing.

'When are you going to move into town? You'd be much more comfortable. And we could see each other more often.'

'Celia, you know I can't leave Arden Gate. Not . . . not since Father had to leave . . .'

'Rosalind, don't tell me again your father was innocent. He was caught with my father's cattle on Arden Gate

17

range. Father had to send Sheriff Porter after him. I know he's hiding out in the hills. Rumour has it he has gathered a gang of desperadoes around him. Father says it is your father's band of rustlers that makes night raids on his herds.'

'Dear Celia, let's not fall out over the things our fathers do or did not do. And you know I can't leave here. Your father wants this ranch. While I stay on here he can't take it over. Some day I hope to prove my father's innocence and then he can return and run his ranch the way he always did. In the meantime you are the only friend I have. And while I do appreciate your generosity I value more our friendship.'

'You're a stupid, stubborn strip of jerky, Rosalind Pond. I don't know why I bother with you. If you weren't so big and dumb, I'd chuck you in the back of my gig and take you into town myself. Which reminds me. And I won't take no for an answer. The Big Travelling Show is coming to town tonight and you're coming, like it or not'

4

The town of Henderson looked deserted. The usually bustling streets were empty and many stores had CLOSED notices on them. Down in South Meadows a gay assembly of colourful marquees and booths had sprung up in the night like mushrooms in a paddock. It was here that the citizens of the town and surrounding area now thronged.

The place was a heady mix of noise and gaiety. A steam-organ blared out popular tunes. Showmen called to the crowds to come and sample the delights of the manifold booths. Children yelled and screamed and ran wild through the wonderland of noise and excitement. Handsome females in their Sunday finery strolled with beau or husband through the magic village of brightly coloured canvas. The crowded field radiated with an atmosphere of lively noise and cheerfulness.

The biggest crowd stood by a large marquee. A sign on the tent invited all to pit their fighting skills against John Charles – the undefeated champion of the United States of America. An amazing sum of $500 was on offer to the man who could stay upright in the ring for three rounds.

Celia and Rosalind pushed through the crowd, or rather, pushed after Henry, the groom. Her father had insisted on Henry chaperoning his daughter to the fair. Henry was not the brightest of young men but he was totally devoted to the daughter of his employer. Abuse him as she would, he took it all and worshipped Celia with doglike devotion.

'I don't think it proper for young ladies to see no boxing,' he protested when Celia told him where they wanted to go.

'Henry, since when did you ever think? Just do as you are told and get us in to see the fight.'

The boxing marquee was packed. The crowd was agog as it watched a young man being carried from the raised ring. The reigning champion strutted around the ring raising his fists to the crowd. He was stripped to the waist. Knots of muscle writhed like live things on his arms and shoulders. His large skull was shaved and he looked as though he was carved from a piece of ivory.

'A big round of applause for plucky Joe Hitchens.' The compère held an arm in the general direction of the unconscious form of the young man being ferried from the ring. 'As soon as our champion gets his breath he'll be ready for the next contestant.'

The crowd roared and yelled and stamped on the floorboards.

'Get us closer, stupid boy. We want to see the contestants.'

Thus admonished, Henry pushed his huge form into the crowd. He finished up next to the ring. Sitting on a long bench were four young bruisers waiting their turn to face the champion.

'The next fight is about to start, ladies and gentlemen.'

A young man dressed in farm clothes stepped up to the ringside. The compère bent towards him and quizzed him.

'A big hand for Harvey Mitchell.'

The young man jumped into the ring, red-faced. He was grinning sheepishly as his friends yelled out encouragement.

'Put him to sleep, Harvey.'

'We'll help you spend the five hundred.'

Rosalind looked along the row of waiting contenders. Something about one young man held her attention. She could not take her eyes off the good-looking boy. Beside her Celia was jumping up and down with excitement.

'Celia, you see that young fella sitting towards the end?'

Celia looked where her friend was pointing.

'So?'

'Don't you think he's very good-looking?'

'For God's sake, Rosalind, he might look all right now but his face will be a mess by the time he is carried from the ring.'

The sound of a bell drew their attention back to the fight. Harvey was squaring up to the champion. He was still grinning self-consciously when John Charles hit him. When he bounced from the ropes the champion hit him again. Harvey stretched out on the floor of the ring, unmoving. A roar came from the crowd. Two derby-hatted assistants ducked into the ring and dragged the unconscious boy out to the side.

Rosalind was tugging at Henry's sleeve. He turned his big, bovine eyes on her.

'Henry, see that young man, second from the end. Go tell him not to fight.'

'Rosalind, have you gone crazy?' Celia was glaring at her tall friend.

'I . . . I . . . Oh Celia, I don't want to see him hurt.'

The look of disgust on Celia's face told what she thought of her friend's sentiments.

'Go on, Henry. Please tell him.'

The girls watched Henry push through the crowd. Impulsively Rosalind followed. Celia was forced to tag along. Rosalind could hear her muttering behind her. As the girls approached, Henry was pointing them out to the young man.

Owen looked in bewilderment at the girls. To the best of his knowledge he had never seen either of them. The tall auburn-haired girl smiled timidly at him.

'Have you told him, Henry?' Rosalind asked nervously.

'I told him, Miss Rosalind.'

Owen looked into the deep-green eyes and was speechless.

'You'll not fight, then?'

'I . . . I must fight, miss. I put my name down.'

There was another animal roar from the crowd and the next bout was concluded. The burly man on the end rose to go to the ring and Owen was next in line.

'Please, for my sake, don't do it,' Rosalind pleaded.

'For God's sake, take no notice of her,' Celia interrupted. 'She was kicked in the head by a mule when she was five years old and she's never been right since. Just you get into that ring and punch that John Charles into the middle of next week.'

Rosalind and Owen were staring at each other as if they were all alone in the marquee. Owen opened his mouth to say something but nothing came out. The howl from the crowd indicated the defeat of another contestant. It was Owen's turn to fight. He could hear someone calling him.

'Come on, sonny. Or are you goin' to chicken out.'

5

Owen allowed himself to be led to the ring. The compère leaned towards him.

'What name?'

'Owen Lismore.'

There was a sudden glint in the compère's eye. He turned to the champion, who was strutting around shaking his fist at the crowd and scowling. Some people were yelling abuse at the boxer and others were calling encouragement to the youngster clambering into the ring.

'Owen Lismore,' the compère yelled out. 'A big hand for Owen, folks.'

Obediently the crowd yelled and clapped for the new contestant. Owen was dressed in a light cotton shirt. It was very loose-fitting and was open to his belly, showing a well-muscled torso.

'You need to be free to move,' Adam had advised. 'Wear my shirt. It too big but not restrict you move about. And remember – don't mix! If I know dis John Charles, I guess he'll be out of condition and over-confident. So you must box him. Wear him down. He get winded and want to finish you quick. Doan let him close. He mangle you in the clinches. Remember all I tell you, boy, and remember you must box. Doan let him in close. You only got to last dree rounds.'

The crowd was roaring at the fighters. Owen balled his fists and tried to concentrate. A pair of emerald-green eyes kept intruding on his vision. And then he was lying on his back staring up at the marquee roof and wondering for a moment how he had got to be lying on the floor.

He turned his head and saw the booted foot coming. The hours of constant training with Adam paid off and he rolled hard and fast to one side, coming up to his knees and shaking his head to clear it. For the next few moments he was busy as he ducked and weaved to keep out of danger. Even so a haymaker caught him on the side of the head, momentarily dazing him.

He back-pedalled furiously, ducked under another punch and drove a hard right into the exposed ribs. His punch was hard and fast. He put all his strength and skill into the effort. He felt something give under the power of his strike. The big, shaven-headed fighter winced and doubled over. Owen moved in to strike again. Something hit him on the back and a foot kicked his ankle. Again the hours of training paid off. Instead of tripping up Owen sidestepped and some quick footwork brought him around behind John Charles.

In his mind was the thought that the compère must have accidentally bumped against him. He glanced over at the referee and caught the venomous look from the man's scowling face. Suddenly Owen realized he was fighting two opponents. Then he was occupied with fending off another assault from the champion. Quick footwork took him out of danger. He saw an opening and swiftly his fist lashed out and caught John Charles in the ear. The big man roared angrily and suddenly charged at the youngster. Owen tried to back away. Again the compère obstructed him.

As he tried to disentangle himself from between the two men, John Charles was on top of him. With a quick movement the bruiser had him in a bear-grip. Owen punched hard inside the clinch. Without warning he saw stars as a forehead crashed into his face. He cried out in agony. Blood cascaded from his nose. Sudden pain jarred up from his groin as a hard knee jerked into him. Just in time Owen pushed his face into the sweaty chest of his opponent as the forehead came down again. There was a grunt from the big fighter as his own nose bashed against the top of Owen's skull.

The youngster relaxed his body and allowed his knees to go slack. The unexpected move caught John Charles by surprise as he tried to hold onto the sweaty youngster. Owen suddenly straightened up and the top of his head connected hard against a projecting chin. He began to push hard against John Charles. His opponent gave ground, lost his footing and fell back. Owen landed on top. The fierce grip slackened and he managed to roll to safety. He saw the trouser-clad legs of the compère advancing towards him.

With sudden fury he drove his fist into the man's knee. His hand hurt from the punch but there was a satisfying crack and a scream. He saw the referee topple to the floor, gripping his damaged knee. The man was screaming and thrashing about in agony. Owen saw no more for a pair of brawny arms wrapped around his body from behind. His arms were trapped inside a rib-crushing grip. Slowly the grip tightened. Owen had difficulty in breathing. The referee, seeing what was happening to the youngster, ceased his screaming and crawled towards the helpless Owen, intent on revenge.

Trying his earlier ploy, the youngster let his body sag. John Charles was expecting the move and held firm – taking the youngster's weight. Owen was unsure of his next move. Then he realized that the referee, crawling towards him, could be a real danger.

John Charles was hugging him hard and his ribs were hurting. Trying to ignore the pain Owen concentrated on the referee. When the man was within range he kicked out hard and sure.

The toe of his boot smashed into the referee's nose. Blood spurted immediately from the crushed organ. The referee opened his mouth to start screaming again. A boot smashed into his chin, snapping shut his teeth. The man rolled to one side, his hands clasping his ruined jaw. He was making animal-like mewling sounds. Losing all interest in the fighting he crawled towards the side of the ring leaving a smear of blood in his wake.

Owen's tactics were seriously worrying his captor, for the champion attempted to swing him out of range of the injured compère. The youngster immediately drove his heel hard into John Charles's instep and pushed in the direction of the swing. It was enough to unbalance the pair.

Again they toppled to the floor. The brawny arms holding him cushioned Owen's fall. Unfortunately for his opponent they went down on the champion's elbow. Owen sensed the bone give. There was a gasp of pain from behind him and the crushing grip was released. Owen rolled away from the danger.

He was breathing hard. Blood poured in rivulets from his mouth and nose. His ribs hurt and his lungs were on fire. He forced himself to his feet. Before him a figure swayed. Owen surged forward. His work-hardened fists smashed into flesh.

Again and again he struck. A blind rage overcame him. He felt his fists striking home and he relished every blow. Then his opponent was on his knees. Owen blinked in surprise. He drew back his right. The fist thudded into John Charles's head. The undefeated champion of the

United States of America hit the floor. He was out cold. An unknown young cowpuncher had put the champion on the canvas. The crowd went wild.

6

Three men in derby hats and waistcoats were clambering into the ring. Owen tried a grin with his bruised and bleeding lips. He gave up, as it was too painful. These men were the officials who kept order in the boxing booth. He relaxed. The prize of $500 was in the bag.

They were burly men with faces that had taken much pummelling during their lifetimes. Flattened noses and scars spoke much of a career in brawling. They reached the young winner. One grabbed his arms. The second punched Owen hard in the stomach while the third one punched him in the ear. The youngster gasped and doubled forward, restrained from hitting the floor only by arms of the first pug. Again a fist crashed into the side of his head.

These men were under the orders of the injured referee to finish the new champion. Another fist in the head and Owen saw stars. He tried to fight back. It was a hopeless cause. Exhausted by his bout with John Charles, Owen was in no state to take on three experienced brawlers.

Rosalind watched in disbelief as the men attacked Owen. Her relief at the young man's victory had been short-lived. In the front row she had watched the young-ster's brave fight with a pounding heart. When the

28

compère had joined in the fight she had wanted to get up in the ring with him and help. A young woman of impulse, she now pushed forward and gripped the edge of the ring in an effort to climb into the arena. An arm grabbed her.

'What the hell are you thinking?' Celia hissed.

'We've got to help him!' Rosalind looked wildly at her tiny friend.

For a moment Rosalind thought Celia was going to have a fit. Her face twisted up into a ferocious grimace that only Celia could achieve. Rosalind was taken aback. Then in a piercing voice Celia screamed.

The scream cut out into the crowd like a bugle-call. Most of the men in the crowd liked to think they were the protectors of the gentler sex. The sound of a female in distress immediately grabbed their attention. Celia's voice rang out, clarion-clear, into the hushed crowd.

'My brother! The dirty rats are trying to kill him! They don't want to pay him the prize-money. Help my poor, brave brother!'

Celia turned and gripped her chaperon by the lapels of his jacket.

'Henry, you great, lumbering pachyderma, get up in that ring and help that poor boy.'

Henry had no idea what a pachyderm was, but it sounded pretty good. His great hands gripped the side of the ring and he heaved himself up. Others, seeing Henry's action, pressed forward. They surged up and into the ring and surrounded the battling trio.

Henry got there first. His great, hamlike fist connected with the first pugilist. The man staggered to one side and grabbed the ropes to stop himself from falling. Then the crowd was swarming through the ring, kicking and punching the officials.

Owen had almost lost consciousness as he sank under

the rain of blows from his attackers. He felt strong hands grip his shoulders and then he was being dragged away. He did not see what was happening in the ring as the derby-hatted men were beaten and kicked by an angry mob.

Sections of the crowd, battling to get at the action, began fighting amongst themselves. Just as Henry dragged Owen down onto the floor the ring collapsed under the weight of men now brawling with anyone and everyone. Men went down in sprawling heaps. In the main body of the marquee, gangs of fighting men swayed backwards and forwards. A supporting pole snapped as a gang of fighters surged against it.

'Get us out of here!' Celia screamed at Henry.

Dragging Owen by an arm and a leg Henry ploughed through the crowd of rioters. As he was dragged along the ground Owen was trying to protest at this undignified method of transport. Henry took no notice. He had been instructed to rescue the young fighter and he had been told to get out. His huge frame elbowed battling men out of the way as he made for the exit.

The canvas marquee swayed alarmingly. Support-poles were snapping all around the tent. Some of the fighters were trying to free the wooden poles to use as weapons. The girls kept behind Henry as he blundered through the crowd.

They fought their way into the open with Owen desperately trying to catch the attention of his rescuer. Henry dragged him clear of the marquee. Behind them the marquee slowly subsided. Men were yelling and still fighting inside as the canvas settled around them. The shouts became muffled but the fighting still went on. Someone had the idea of cutting his way out. Dozens of knives appeared as everyone cottoned on to this new development. Soon a wholesale butchering of the canvas was in progress.

'Home, Henry, home!' yelled Celia.

Still dragging his charge, Henry started for the Duke residence. Owen groaned as he was dragged over the ground, gathering dust and mud and more bruises in the process. He gave up trying to protest and resigned himself to his fate.

7

Adam did not need the voice to tell him not to move. The cold, round object pressing into his ear was warning enough.

'You stir a finger, Swede and you're dead. This little ol' Colt'll blow your putrid little brain out your other ear-hole.'

Adam kept very still. He knew quite well to whom the voice belonged.

'Slowly, but slowly, you roll over onto your big fat belly. I cleaned out these Swede-blasters real good.'

Obediently Adam rolled over.

'Put your hands behind your back – real careful now.'

A rope was draped round his neck and then taken down around his wrists. He gasped as the rope tightened. A gun barrel jolted across the back of his head.

'That's just a taste of what's in store, Swede, if you don't do as you're told.'

'Doan hurt me, boss,' Adam whined. 'I haven't do nothing.' Adam was aware a man's guard dropped if he thought the victim was too frightened to fight back. 'I do what you tell me.'

'You'll help, you bastard, if you know what's good for you. Nobody hits Josh Bassinet.'

Again the gun barrel crashed into the side of Adam's

head. He gritted his teeth against the pain.

'Oooh . . . doan hit me, boss, I do what you want. I sorry I hit you. I doan know what came over me.'

'I ain't about to kill you yet, you piece of shit. If you do what you're told I might just let you live.'

'Get him over here on this straw,' another voice intervened.

Hands gripped him and Adam was propped up against a straw bale. He looked up into the faces of Oliver Lismore and Josh Bassinet.

'Now, where's young Owen got to?'

'Owen? Ain't he back yet?'

The gun barrel hit him across the forehead with such force it split the skin. His head rocked back and blood seeped down his face.

'I ask the questions. You just answer them, Swede. Now let's start again. Where's Owen?'

Adam shook his head to clear it. 'Honest to God, boss, I doan know. He went into town this morning. I doan seen him since.'

'This is one thick Swede. I don't think he knows a thing.'

Oliver gave his prisoner a brutal kick.

'Goddamn his Swede heart. We know Owen survived the boxing but after that he seems to have disappeared. We should have gone ourselves to the fight to make sure.'

'You know we couldn't be involved. We had to be seen in the saloon, playing cards while the fight was on.'

'We know he didn't collect the prize-money so he'll come back here. He has no place else to go. There's only one trail into Ayli from town. Why don't we lie in wait and take him as he comes home. He won't suspect anything.'

'Damn you, Josh, he can't be killed near here. I can't have suspicion fall on me.'

'From what I hear tell, those show people have every

33

reason to lay for him and finish him off. He beat their champion and destroyed their tent. Damn well put them out of business. They got so mad they followed him from town and finished him off. We heard the racket and dashed out to see what was the trouble. We manage to chase them off and find Owen bad hurt. Afore he dies he tells us who it was that done for him.'

A slow smile crossed Oliver's handsome face. 'Son of a bitch, Josh, that's a damn fine tale you tell. It could just work.'

'What about the Swede? Shall I finish him off?'

Bassinet lifted the Colt and aimed it at the injured man lying at his feet.

'Wait a minute, Josh, one thing at a time. Leave him here. He's not going anywhere hogtied like that. Later tonight this old barn goes on fire and in the morning we find a body all burned up. No bullet holes – no questions.'

After some more brutal kicking the plotters left the barn. A low groan came from the bruised and bloody figure on the floor. 'Look like Owen won dat fight after all. Now it up to ol' Adam here to find a way to save the boy from dat no good pair.'

Painfully he began to work on his bonds. Every movement was agony. From time to time he groaned and rested from his struggles but then doggedly carried on struggling with the rope.

During the beating, as his body had cringed against the brutal blows, the rope around his neck had tightened. There were red, bloody weals on his throat where the rope had rubbed his neck raw. It was a painful and painstaking task.

Then his hands were free and he was able to pull the rope from his neck. He crawled towards the door. He was used to sleeping out in the barn. Indeed, Oliver had insisted on this arrangement. No amount of pleading by

34

Owen would change Oliver's treatment of the big cowpuncher.

Adam pushed at the large wooden doors of the barn. It was still dark outside. Adam figured it was late in the evening. Everything was quiet. Using the door as a prop Adam got to his feet. He staggered across the paddock and made his way up to the ranch house. The place looked deserted and there were no lights on in the house.

'I guess dat pair is out on the road waiting for Owen,' he muttered. 'I know exactly where dey is at.'

He stumbled up to the back door and almost fell over the threshold. When he emerged into the night he had a pistol-belt strapped round his waist and was carrying a long-barrelled rifle. He sat on the porch step and thought things out. At last he struggled to his feet and shuffled to the stables.

As he saddled up, waves of dizziness swept over him. When that happened he had to stop and lean his head against the side of the horse.

8

'You can't keep a man in your room. Your father will go mad.'

'What else can we do, Rosalind? It was your idea to rescue the creature.'

'He's not a creature. He's a human being. And he needs help.'

Owen decided to stay on the floor of the hallway where the hulking Henry had deposited him. His experience with women was virtually non-existent. He did not know how to react to the argument going on over his head. However it gave him a certain pleasant satisfaction to rest and listen to the girls argue over his fate. He lay with half-closed eyes watching the tall girl with the green eyes. He decided he had never seen anyone so beautiful.

'If we stand here arguing then it will be taken out of our hands when Father returns.'

The girls turned their attention to the battered youth.

'Do you think you can make it up the stairs?'

Owen nodded eagerly – then wished he hadn't. The broken glass inside got shaken up and he felt his skull being lacerated. He groaned and lay back again.

'Come on, you poor thing. We'll help you.'

In spite of his sorry condition the sensation of being helped to his feet and supported by the two females was exquisite. With one on each side he almost forgot his injuries.

Owen was surprised at how strong the girls were. Quickly they hauled him upstairs and into a room containing a large bed. Owen had never seen anything so elegant. Flowered drapes hung at the windows. He was utterly fascinated by the matching wallpaper. The floor was carpeted and he was amazed at how soft it felt underfoot. He was led over to the bed and told to sit down. Suddenly he was aware of his filthy condition.

'Oh no, miss, I couldn't.'

The smaller of the girls placed her hand on his chest and pushed him. Taken by surprise he fell back on the bed. The room rocked alarmingly.

'Let's get some of that blood off him.'

Celia walked to a small table and poured water from a large pitcher into a basin. A mixture of embrarrassment and pleasure overwhelmed Owen as the girls used flannels to wash him. Rosalind worked on his face while Celia attended the blood and dirt on his arms and hands. It was almost worth getting a punching, he was thinking.

He tried to watch Rosalind without seeming to. For her part, when she caught his eye she would smile shyly while continuing with her ministrations. Owen was slowly drifting in an ocean of pleasure when there was a commotion from downstairs. The girls looked at each with some alarm.

'Father,' squeaked Celia. 'If he finds us like this there'll be hell to pay. Quick, get rid of the water and dirty flannels. I'll try and keep him from coming up here.'

With quick, agitated movements Celia left the room. Rosalind looked around wildly for a moment and then went into flurry of action. She opened the window and slung the dirty water outside. The soiled flannels and towels were hurriedly pushed under the bed. Then she looked at Owen sitting up and watching her.

'In the bed,' she ordered him.

He stared blankly at her.

'Oh! Stand up!'

Obediently he stood and she whipped the covers back, then pushed him unceremoniously into the bed. He saw no more for she drew the covers up over him.

There were footsteps on the stairs and angry voices.

'Father, do you not believe your own daughter?'

'I believe you, but Sheriff Porter has a warrant for the fella's arrest. He claims he was seen coming in here with you and that Pond girl. I told the sheriff he could look for himself.'

'If Sheriff Porter spent more time at law enforcement than down at the Lucky Star I'd be more impressed. Why does he have to pester innocent citizens instead of finding those villains down at that boxing show?'

'It's the showpeople as made the complaint. They claim this fella, Lismore, tried to kill John Charles, the champion and then started a riot. He then went on to wreck the show tent. Sheriff Porter has a warrant for his arrest.'

'What!' The screech could only have come from Celia. 'You stupid, bumbling old fart.'

Another voice cut in. 'Now, now, Miss Celia, there's no need to abuse the law. I'm only doing my duty. I have to follow up these things. I wouldn't be doing my duty if I didn't.'

'Is doing your duty harassing young ladies in their private apartments?' Celia's voice rose in pitch as she made her protests.

'Celia! That's enough! It's not much to ask you to let the sheriff look in your room. Just stand aside and let us through.'

'I tell you there's no one in there . . .' and then the door was pushed open.

Leonard Duke pushed his head inside his daughter's room and stared at the figure in the bed.

'You! What the hell are you doing here?'

Rosalind blinked owlishly as Sheriff Porter stuck his curious head inside. She slowly sat up. The covers slipped and bare shoulders were exposed.

'Wha . . . what's happening? I remember feeling faint and then I don't remember anything more.'

The sheriff was gawking at Rosalind's naked shoulders. She suddenly realized her condition and pulled the covers back over herself.

'Pa, get that dirty old man out of my bedroom,' squealed Celia. 'I'm sorry, Rosalind, they insisted on barging in here.'

'Get out, Porter,' snarled Duke.

The sheriff's mouth closed abruptly as Leonard Duke elbowed him out of the room.

'And you, young hussy, get dressed and get out of this house immediately.' His eyes took on a mean glint. 'Before you leave I have something to tell you. So come down to my study when you're decent.'

Owen lay in the bed his senses reeling. Not only was the bed scented but a partially undressed Rosalind was lying on top of him. His body began to react to her presence. He tried to sink further back in the mattress in the vain hope that the girl did not notice him. As he drew back so she seemed to press harder down on him. He tried not to moan aloud.

9

The horse plodded along the darkened road. Owen was content to allow it to dawdle. He was on his way home and he did not care much for arriving there. A great deal had happened to him since he had set out for town that morning with such high hopes. He had defeated the champion and been cheated out of his winnings. But above that gloomy memory was the recollection of a tall, beautiful girl with green eyes and auburn hair.

In spite of his disappointment in missing out on the boxing prize, there was a faint glow of contentment and even happiness in his mind. Over and over again he relived the moment when Rosalind had shrugged off her dress and clambered into the bed on top of him. Even the remembrance of his physical discomfiture could not dim the memory of her soft body crushing him down into the mattress.

'Rosalind, fair Rosalind.' The memory of her pale, creamy skin played like fever in his brain. 'I love you, Rosalind.'

Celia had soon shattered his feeling of well-being.

'Come on, you got to get out of here. You heard what the sheriff said. He's got a warrant for you. Father will hound him till he takes you in. He has to do whatever Pa tells him.'

He had been bundled out through the bedroom window. There had been no fond farewells. Rosalind had disappeared down to Mr Duke's study to take whatever he had to tell her. Henry collected Owen's mount from the livery where he had stabled it that morning. The bemused youngster rode out of town, keeping his hat pulled low and taking a roundabout route to get on the road that led to the Ayli.

He saw the horse standing by the side of the trail. It was busy grazing. Then he saw the dark form lying on the road.

'What the hell!'

He spurred forward. The grazing horse lifted its head and watched him ride up. Owen saw someone stretched out in the road. He leapt from the mount and knelt beside the body.

'Hi fella, you hurt or what?'

Gently he lifted the man's head then gasped as he recognized him. The face was so bruised and swollen it was difficult to realise this was his friend and mentor.

'Jeez, Adam, what the hell's happened.' A groan answered him. 'Oh, God, Adam, don't worry. I'll get you home. Just you hang on there.'

He felt totally helpless. There was not even water to give his injured friend.

'Owen . . . dat you. . . ?'

'Sure thing, Adam. Can you ride or will I go on and bring back a wagon for you?'

'Doan . . . go home, boy. Dey waiting for you . . .'

'What is it Adam? Who's waiting? Is it the law?'

'No, not the law, boy . . . Oliver and Josh . . . wait for you. Dey bushwhack you.'

'Adam, who did this?'

'Your brudder and dat gun-slick, Bassinet – dey beat me to tell where you was at. I could tell nothing. I hear tell you

41

done good. You beat dat John Charles. But you can't go home. You'll have to go back the town.'

'Hell, Adam, I can't go back there. Sheriff Porter has a warrant. Figures I wrecked the boxing-booth.'

There was the faint glint of white teeth in the battered face. 'You sure one hellcat, Master Owen.'

Owen thought for a moment. 'What we gonna do, Adam? I gotta get help for you.'

'Doan worry 'bout me, I can ride, I reckon. We'll head into Arden. We can hide out dere and I mend some.'

'Arden! It's a wilderness out there. And it's filled with outlaws and bad 'uns.'

'Dey any worse dan the folk we leave behind? Jus' you help me on my horse.'

Rosalind Pond sat across the desk from Leonard Duke, her face drained of colour. Duke's face was expressionless as he gazed back at the girl. He was a big man with cropped greying hair. His complexion was florid and there was the hint of grey stubble on his cheeks and chin. His eyes were slightly protruding which gave him a somewhat shifty appearance. Before him on the desk was a sheaf of papers.

'So you see, Miss Pond. I have bought the notes your father took out on Arden Gate. Technically the ranch is mine. I intend to run it as a going concern. It has to start making me some money. I'm putting a foreman and crew out there to run things. I want you moved out from the house in the next couple of days.'

'Never! You'll have to kill me first.'

'Dear me, Miss Pond, how melodramatic! You can make this hard or easy. I'm sending a crew out there in the next few days. The men I employ are no concern of mine. I just require them to do a good job. They're a rough bunch. I can't guarantee how they'll behave when they find a lone woman living out there. For your own safety I suggest you are gone before they arrive.' He paused a moment. 'You get my meaning?'

'You are a snake in a suit. I never doubted my father was right when he told me you framed him over those stolen cattle. You've managed to drive out every decent man in this valley. Now you've sunk so low you are making war on women. Some day you'll push the wrong man and he'll drive you back into whatever reptile pit you crawled out of.'

Duke's fist crashed down on the papers. The sudden noise made Rosalind jump. The man across the desk was trembling with fury.

'You hussy! How dare you speak to me like that! You're like your father – no-good trash. You get out of that house or I won't be responsible for what happens to you.'

Quaking inside, Rosalind stood up. Without another word she turned and walked to the door.

'And another thing – I don't want you seeing my daughter again. You've caused her enough grief as it is.'

The girl's look was filled with contempt when she turned back from the door. 'I wonder how Celia, could have been fathered by someone like you. She's got nothing of your poisonous nature.' She slammed the door behind her.

10

'Is there anything else I can do, Miss Celia?'

Henry had just assisted the battered young fighter on his way. As always, eager to please his employer's daughter, he waited her instructions. Before she could answer the slamming of doors within the house distracted her. She turned quizzical eyes towards the rear door and sure enough Rosalind emerged. She watched bemused as her friend slammed the door behind her.

'I thought I was supposed to be the grumpy one,' she observed, highly amused by her friend's uncharacteristic behaviour. When she saw Rosalind's face she stopped being amused. 'What did my father say to you?' she asked uneasily.

Rosalind pushed past her friend. 'Where's my horse?'

But Celia was not so easily brushed aside. 'What did he say to you?'

Rosalind kept her back to her friend as she answered. 'Your father is kicking me out of Arden Gate. Somehow he has gained possession. Also he told me not to see you again.'

When Rosalind turned to face her friend she could see only her back as Celia fled into the house.

'Get my horse, will you, Henry?'

Henry did not get very far. He stopped to listen. The howls of rage from inside the house didn't sound quite human. He looked at Rosalind. Rosalind looked at him. There was no mistaking Celia raving.

'I guess I'd better go, Henry, if you don't mind. Me being here will only make matters worse.'

When Rosalind rode out of the yard the yelling from inside the house seemed, if possible, even louder. She rode towards Arden Gate full of foreboding.

Her inclination was to barricade herself inside her house and fight off Duke's men. But she realized the futility of one lone girl against the crew that would be sent to take over her father's place. She could think of no one who could help her. Over a period of time all her father's friends had been driven from their holdings or had died attempting to defy Leonard Duke. She thought about the young man they had rescued this afternoon.

'Owen, I suppose you might have helped,' she muttered morosely, but then regretted the thought. She would only draw the young man into a conflict not of his own making. Bitterly she came to the conclusion that she was alone. Even her friend, Celia, was forbidden to see her. With such black thoughts she rode towards home.

As she approached Arden Gate there was very little daylight left. She pulled up and gazed at the dim outlines of the house that was the only home she had ever known. The rumble of wheels on the trail behind puzzled her for a moment. Then she guessed what it was. That would be the chuck wagon with supplies for the crew who were to run her ranch. Anger flared as she realized that Leonard Duke had wasted no time in harassing her.

In spite of her intentions not to resist eviction, this flagrant disregard for her own needs enraged her. She dug her heels into her pony's sides and galloped the last few hundred yards to the house. Inside, it was but a moment's work to grab a box of shells and her rifle and kneel by a window. Levering a shell into the chamber she rested the barrel on the windowsill and awaited the arrival of Leonard Duke's men.

The settling dusk made it difficult to make out details of the vehicle coming towards the house. Rosalind sighted on the horse but knew she could not take out her anger on a dumb animal. The driver was just a dark shape on the wagon seat. Even so she still could not bring herself to shoot without warning. She raised the sights and fired a shot high into the night sky.

The horse whinnied and halted. Someone was yelling but Rosalind could not make out the words.

'Turn that wagon round and go back or the next shot will take your head off. Tell that scabby boss of yours I ain't gone yet and until I do no one's setting foot on Arden Gate property.'

There was enough light for Rosalind to see the driver stand upright in the wagon.

'Rosalind Pond, if you don't stop shooting I'm gonnna come up there and shove that rifle somewhere where it won't see daylight for a month of Sundays.'

Rosalind's jaw dropped in astonishment. 'Celia, is that you?'

'I'm coming up there, so keep your finger off that damn trigger.'

Rosalind walked outside and watched the wagon roll up to the front door. Her friend climbed down and stood gazing at her.

'What the hell do you mean, shooting that damn rifle off at me? I've a good mind to kick that big backside of yours.'

'Oh, Celia . . .' Rosalind hugged her friend in a hard embrace. 'I don't understand. Your father said we weren't to see each other again.'

'Stop messing about, you big slop. Help me in with my things.'

Celia wriggled from the embrace and turned to the buggy.

'Things, what things?'

Suddenly Celia giggled. 'My inheritance. Come on, then. Don't stand there like a half-wit.'

It took a couple of trips to carry the various bundles inside. As Rosalind lit the lamps Celia unpacked her bags. With mounting incomprehension she watched as a nest of necklaces and rings and bejewelled brooches were piled on the table. Small bags of coin joined the collection. Rosalind turned to face her friend.

'Where did all this come from?'

'I told you, it's my inheritance, stupid.'

Celia was glaring at her with that familiar cantankerous look that Rosalind knew so well.

'So tell me what's this all about?'

'Against my better judgement, Rosalind Pond, you and I are in this together.'

'In what together?' Rosalind asked in bewilderment.

'I've left home. I'm coming with you. And don't argue. One word from you and I'll leave immediately and go back home again.'

'Oh, Celia, you don't know what you've done. I have to leave here. Tomorrow I'll be homeless. Don't you understand that?'

'You big buffalo, and who's gonna look after you? You'll never survive on your own. You'll need me to take care of you. So there! You're stuck with me, like it or not.'

Celia stared defiantly at her friend. Rosalind slowly sank onto an old settee. Her face was working. To Celia's amazement big tears swelled in her eyes and poured down her cheeks.

'For God's sake, Rosalind, what the hell's the matter

with you? Stop that bawling at once or . . . or . . . or . . . Oh, damn you, Rosalind Pond, if you ain't the silliest girl I ever did know.'

'I can't help it, Celia. It's all too much for me.' Rosalind's voice was muffled as she mopped at her face with a handkerchief.

'Oh, hell and tarnation, Rosalind, just get those big ungainly bones of yours into that kitchen and get supper ready. All this disaccommodation has given me an appetite.'

11

The first light of morning was teasing at the windows. Rosalind sat up in the bed. It had been a night of fitful sleep. She had tossed and turned as she worried about the future. She looked across at the other bed. A faint snore came from somewhere under the heap of bed covers.

'Oh, Celia,' she whispered, 'I can't say how much it means to me to have you here. I wish it were under happier circumstances. You are a true and steadfast companion. I wonder if you realize what you've let yourself into.'

Carefully she eased herself from the bed and shivered slightly in the crisp air. Later in the day it would get warm but this early in the morning it was still chilly.

In the kitchen she soon had a fire in the stove. Deftly she mixed dough for biscuits and put the pot on for the coffee. The table was laid and the coffee was bubbling on the stove when a tousle-haired Celia poked her head round the kitchen door.

'What the hell time is it? The smell of that coffee woke me. Can't you sleep?'

'Good morning, my bright little morning star. Breakfast is ready when you are.'

'Consarn it, Rosalind, even the hens aren't up yet.' Celia scowled at her friend. 'I hope this early morning lark isn't gonna be a regular habit.'

Nevertheless she came and sat at the table. Rosalind cracked eggs into the pan.

'Have you thought any more on what you'll do?' Celia asked, stirring sugar into her coffee.

Rosalind poured another mug and sat down. 'Yes, I have. I'm going to look for Father.'

Celia's eyes widened. 'Your father! Why, he's somewhere in Arden. You can't go in there. Its full of thieves and outlaws.'

'Oh, Celia, I know. But what else can I do?'

'Two females – alone in Arden! Can you just imagine what those brigands in Arden will do to two young, tasty females? Well, one tasty female and one that looks like a overgrown mule.'

In spite of herself Rosalind laughed out loud. 'Oh, Celia, I'm so glad you are here. I love you dearly.'

'Huh!' Celia snorted and then stopped and looked speculatively at her companion. 'You have just given me an idea. And you're such an ugly cuss you could just do it.'

'Do what?' asked Rosalind through a mouthful of bread.

'As you look like a man, why don't you dress up as one?'

Rosalind almost choked on her biscuit. Quickly she took a gulp of coffee. 'What!'

'You're tall, you're lanky, you're awkward – dressed in man's gear you'd easily be mistaken for a male.'

For moments the girls stared at each other. Then a grin broke across Rosalind's face.

'A husband and wife travelling through Arden, how perfect! Let's do it!' Even as she spoke Rosalind cocked her head. 'Can you hear that? Something's on my porch.' Sudden alarm awakened in her face. 'You don't think . . .'

They both listened. They could hear a shuffling noise and then a couple of grunts.

'Is it an animal or has your pa sent his men after you?' Rosalind whispered. As she spoke she stood and picked up her rifle.

'It can't be Father. No one knows I came out here. He probably hasn't missed me yet.'

The girls tiptoed to the front door. Rosalind cocked her rifle. She nodded to Celia. 'You open the door. Do it quick.'

'Wait.'

Celia rushed back to the stove and picked up a stout metal poker. When she returned she looked apprehensively at her companion. Both girls were tense. Rosalind nodded and the door was whipped open.

They stared with some incomprehension at the bundle on the porch. A large pair of feet jutted from under a horse-blanket. The bundle snorted and shifted. A hand came out and tugged at the blanket. Gingerly Rosalind reached out and poked the bundle with the rifle barrel.

'You there, come out with your hands up. I got a gun here.'

The blanket slid down and a large pair of mulish eyes stared up at them. 'Miss Celia, Miss Rosalind.'

'Henry! What in tarnation are you up to?'

Henry struggled out from under the blanket. He stood before the puzzled girls, his clothes creased and dusty, shifting his big frame awkwardly from one foot to the other.

'Henry, did my father send you to spy on me? I'm going to bash your stupid little brain in with this poker.'

'No, no, Miss Celia, I come of my own account. I thought you might need some help. I was worried when I saw you go off in the buggy last night. So I followed you.'

'You dumb ox! I *am* going to bash you . . .' Celia raised the poker and the big dumb ox cowered before the young woman who looked like a child beside his bulk.

51

'Celia, leave the poor boy alone. Come in, Henry. I suppose you could do with some breakfast?'

Henry's dull face brightened. 'Yes, Miss Rosalind, I sure am hungry.'

'Feed him?' Celia screeched. 'He's not coming in this house.'

Rosalind stepped forward and took the cowering Henry by the arm. 'Come in, Henry. I got some fresh-baked biscuits and eggs. How does that set with you?'

Nodding vigorously Henry allowed himself to be escorted inside. He still cast nervous glances at the glowering Celia but Rosalind guided him to the kitchen table and set him down. She poured fresh coffee and Henry set to as if he had not seen food for a week. The youth stopped eating only when there was nothing left to eat.

'Thank you Miss Rosalind, that was real good.' Henry sat quietly with eyes downcast – his huge hands placed on his knees.

'Now Henry, we have a lot to do today. We need to be getting on with it. So you can go on back to town and tell Mr Duke that Celia is all right'

'I can't do that, Miss Rosalind. Not after Mr Duke said as Miss Celia was not to 'sociate with you no more. He would be very angry if he knew she was out here with you.'

Rosalind frowned. 'Henry, did Mr Duke really send you out here?'

'Oh no, miss, he don't know I'm here. He'll be powerful beside himself when I don't turn up for work this morning.'

'This stupid piece of dung don't know what day it is, Rosalind. I don't know why you're asking him dumb questions. Of course my pa sent him. Why else would he be here?'

'Celia, go in the bedroom and sort out some clothes for that little project we discussed over breakfast.'

Celia opened her mouth to make some protest but stopped when Rosalind vigorously shook her head and pointed in the direction of the bedroom. To her surprise her waspish little friend stomped off with no more than a token snarl at her. She poured their guest another mug of coffee and gently began to probe him as to why he was here at Arden Gate. When she had finished she left the table and went into Celia. Clothes were strewn about the room.

'Did you find anything?' asked Rosalind.

An irritated Celia folded her arms and glared at her. 'Did you find out anything?' she countered.

Rosalind sat on the bed and contemplated her feisty friend. 'Promise me that what I tell you is in strictest confidence and you will never let on to a soul what I am about to tell you.'

'What the hell are you on about?'

'It's no good getting angry with me. I want your word.'

Celia's eyes were glittering with suppressed annoyance. 'My word is my bond,' she said at last, glaring at Rosalind.

Rosalind sighed. 'That big dumb ox, as you are so fond of calling him, is innocent of any subterfuge. That big dumb ox worships the ground you walk on. He followed you last night because he was worried you were in some sort of trouble. He slept out on the porch all last night because he thought that was the best way of protecting you. Short of hitting him over the head with a club and roping him to a fence-post, there is no way of stopping him from accompanying us when we leave here.'

For once Celia was lost for words. She stared at her friend with mouth agape. 'The poor dumb brute,' she said weakly. 'The poor dumb brute.'

12

'Hang on in there, Adam. I'm sure we'll find somewhere soon.'

For two days the fugitives had wandered through the fastness of Arden. Well-marked trails that should have led somewhere petered out after a few miles. Completely lost and without food or water, even Owen's young, healthy constitution was beginning to feel the strain.

He could not remember how many times his friend had fallen from his mount. Now the man lay on the ground and looked grey and drawn. His lips were cracked and broken. Blood had caked on his face, giving him the look of someone with a serious skin disease.

Owen licked his own dry lips. At Adam's suggestion they had tried putting pebbles in their mouths. It worked somewhat on the first day but now on the second day it was no longer effective. They were in a desperate condition. Owen knew they needed to find water and food soon or they would not survive. A low moan from Adam brought his attention back to the condition of his friend.

'Go on, Owen, save yourself. I only holding you back.'

The words were spoken so quietly Owen had to bend low to make out what his friend was saying. In one way he knew Adam was right. The slow progress they were making was an added risk. But Owen knew he could not abandon his friend, no matter the risk to himself.

'Don't worry, Adam, we'll find somewhere soon.'

Owen stared around him seeking inspiration in his surroundings. There was nothing, only barren rock to greet his eyes. Then he noticed the rifle stock protruding from the saddle of Adam's mount. It gave him an idea.

'Rest here awhile, Adam. I'll take the rifle and find us some game. We'll have something to eat at least. And,' he added, more optimistic than he felt, 'where there's game there'll be water.' He slid the rifle from its sheath and checked the load. 'Rest easy, Adam. I'll be back soon with food and water.'

'The mighty hunter goeth forth,' Adam murmured with an attempt at humour.

Owen smiled faintly and began to trudge up the trail they had been following before Adam had fallen that last time from his mount. In spite of Owen's encouragement, the big man insisted he had not the strength to go on.

'I finish, boy. Go on, save yourself. Dat beating broke me. I not got it in me to go no further.'

But Owen could not simply ride away from his friend. He was determined he would find something to save them both. As he trudged up the dusty trail there was very little sign of vegetation or animal life to encourage optimism.

He kept looking at the sun and checking on landmarks. All he needed now was to get lost and then they would both be finished. Wearily he trudged along trying to keep a wary eye out for something that would help them in their desperate plight.

He had always imagined the Arden hills to be populated with outlaws and prospectors. The rocky wilderness was too inaccessible and hostile for lawmen to launch any sort of foray in search of fugitives.

'What I really need now is to find an old prospector with a hoard of grub and a well out the back,' he muttered.

And then he smelt the wood-smoke.

For a few moments he stood sniffing the air, then cautiously he crept forward following his nose. The path led upwards along a narrow, rocky trail. A sudden burst of laughter brought him up sharp. He was close to the source of the fire. Very carefully placing one boot in front of the other he climbed further and was rewarded by seeing the blue smoke from a fire drifting up. On a rocky crest he got down on hands and knees and advanced even more slowly.

There were four of them seated in a circle around a camp-fire. His stomach growled so fiercely he was afraid the men would hear him. He massaged the offending organ in an attempt to quieten it. Someone spoke and provoked another burst of laughter. Owen lay and studied the men.

Three of them were middle-aged, clean-shaven and dressed in patched but serviceable work-shirts and denims. The fourth was a handsome young man who looked the same age as his brother, Oliver. Looking at them he had a hard job picturing them as desperadoes. But he knew that was a mistake. Only bandits and outlaws lived in the wilds of Arden.

They were in the process of cooking a meal. A large pot of stew or beans hung on a tripod, while in the flames a coffee-pot bubbled. The smell of food cooking was overwhelming. Owen felt a wave of weakness as his hunger pinched hard at his insides. He took a deep breath. The men wore side-arms but seemed relaxed and off-guard. Slowly he stood.

'Nobody move! I got you covered!'

The banter in the camp stopped. In slow motion the heads turned towards the youth with the rifle.

'Anyone makes a move and I'll drop you where you sit.'

'It's all right, kid, we ain't about to do anything foolish. Are you the law? You sure don't look like no law. You're too young – unless they's robbing the cradle nowadays.'

'Sure don't look like no law to me, Pete. He looks more like one of them hillbillies that come to buy beeves of us. You from Eden, kid? You one of them there Children of Paradise?'

'If you looking to rob us, kid, we got no money. We put all our capital in livestock.'

Somehow this remark amused the men. They chortled some but stayed relaxed. Owen was disconcerted. He expected a certain amount of surliness and at least some resistance. These men sat around the camp and spoke casually as if they were used to being held up by a wild, gun-toting kid every other day.

'I'm warning you. Move back from that fire and sit facing me in a row.'

Obediently the outlaws did as they were told, shuffling around to face Owen.

'You think he's gonna shoot us, Marvin?'

'Sure looks like it – lining us all up like this. Have we done something to you in the past, kid? Is this a revenge raid or what?'

Owen clambered down to their level. They sat complacently observing him. Their calmness was unnerving.

'I'm gonna take this pot of stew off the fire. My finger's on the trigger. If anyone does anything foolish I won't be responsible for what happens.' Owen crouched by the fire, trying to keep the rifle on the men, and reached forward to the pot.

'Don't touch that pot, kid!'

Owen jerked in surprise. This was the first indication of resistance from the bandits. His rifle wavered.

'I told you! Don't move! I'm taking this here pot.' He grabbed the handle of the pan and jerked back abruptly as the hot metal burnt his fingers. 'Goddamn it!' he yelled. 'Goddamn it!'

Forgetting to keep the rifle on the bandits, Owen cursed and frantically waved his hand in the air in a vain attempt to ease the excruciating pain. Just in time he remembered the dangerous foursome he was confronting. To his amazement they were still sitting where he had told them to sit and regarding him curiously.

'I did try to warn you, kid,' one of the men remarked mildly.

'You reckon on stealing our food? Hell, boy, are you just hungry?'

Owen looked at the man who had spoken. He had a pleasant, square face with swept-back dark hair. Still nursing his blistered hand Owen nodded.

'I ain't ate in two or three days.' Owen couldn't remember when he'd had his last meal.

'Christ, kid, if that's all you want, you welcome to join us.'

A burly man with dark, swarthy skin moved to the fire and picked up an iron hook. Ignoring the youth with the rifle he deftly plucked the pot from the tripod. 'Dig out an extra dish, Jack,' he called over his shoulder. 'And while you're at it bring some bear-grease for the kid's hand.'

The young, good-looking one got up from the line of men and after rummaging about came up with a stack of tin plates.

'You sure are welcome to join us, kid. We was about to eat, anyway.'

Owen looked down at his swelling, blistered hand. He blew on the burnt fingers while he thought about what was happening. He was completely at a loss. While he sat regarding his injured members, the men gathered round the fire to partake in the shared-out food. Owen felt very foolish. Sheepishly he set his rifle on the ground beside him. The man with the jar of bear-grease squatted beside him and began to smear some of the mess on his blisters.

'That's gonna hurt for a day or two. The only remedy we have for pain is rot-skull. You're welcome to try some of that.'

I . . . I'm sorry I threw down on you. I thought you was bandits.'

His remarks amused the men squatting by the fire. They gave sideways glances and grinned at some secret joke.

'Here, kid.' The burly man handed a heaped plate to Owen.

'I . . . can't . . . not yet, anyways. I have a friend back down the trail in a bad way. I'll have to fetch him up here if you won't mind.'

'Mind! Hell, kid, I'll come and help you. Don't you fellas eat all that there grub. Me and the kid here will be back in a jiffy.'

13

'I can go no further, Rosalind. I just want to lie down here and die. Put on my tombstone – here lies a lonely lass, who expired from fatigue in this barren pass.'

'Oh, Celia how many times have I to remind you? My name is Giles. Rosalind I abandoned back at Arden Gate.'

Celia looked at the tall, good-looking youth atop his mount. Rosalind had made an outfit out of a mixture of old work-wear and some of her absent father's clothes. They had used make-up Celia had brought from home to give her fair skin a tanned look. Underneath the low-brimmed hat Celia knew her friend's hair had been cropped short. Rosalind had agonized over the butchery of her long auburn hair.

'It's got to go,' Celia had insisted, 'if you are to carry off this substitution.'

Not being skilled in haircutting Celia's fmished effect was far from edifying. Celia had collapsed with mirth at the horrified look on Rosalind's face when she viewed the end result in the large mirror in the bedroom.

'Oh, my God! I look like an escapee from a lunatic asylum!'

By then Celia was unable to make any cogent rejoinder, having crawled onto the bed and buried her face in the coverings. Even now the memory of it brought a smile to her face. She tried to suppress the tendency to show any hint of cheeriness and instead glared at her friend.

'And how many times do I have to remind you, my name is not Celia, but Abigail.'

'You're right, Abigail,' Rosalind said wearily. 'Perhaps we'll find a place to stop soon.'

There was a clatter of hoofs and Henry cantered back down the trail towards them.

'Looks like some buildings up ahead. About a mile up this trail.'

'Civilization at last,' Celia responded. 'Let's hope that there's a decent hotel.'

The dogs rushed in a pack down the track towards them, barking furiously. They fought to keep the horses from bolting while yelling at the hounds to back off. Celia had refused to be parted from her riding-quirt and she laid about the mongrels with an enthusiasm that belied her weariness moments before. Cowed but not defeated the noisy animals accompanied them to the outskirts of a jumble of dilapidated buildings. In spite of the presence of the boisterous dogs the place seemed deserted.

'Hallo there!' Henry bellowed. 'Anyone at home?'

Not daring to face the ferocious dogs on foot they stayed mounted and stared round with some curiosity at the ramshackle dwellings.

Long rows of shabby vegetables were set out in patches of cultivated ground. A few fruit-bushes and apple-trees grew behind the shacks. Untidy stacks of cut timber cluttered the space between the dwellings. Broken carts stood with shafts jutting into the air like spindly limbs upraised in prayer. Old barrels and rusting machinery added to the general air of dilapidation and neglect.

The men appeared then – a silent appearance from nowhere. One moment the place was deserted, then the menacing ragamuffin figures stepped out from behind buildings and fences. Without exception they all carried long mountain rifles. These were pointing at the trio of newcomers.

A coarse, greasy-haired stump of a man stepped forward. His hair was long and unwashed and hung in tails to his shoulders. His brutal face was swarthy and darkened even further by several days' growth of stubble. Greasy clothing clung to his muscular frame as if stuck to him with layers of animal fat and dirt. He kept his rifle pointed at Henry.

'What you want?' The voice had the timbre of a file being dragged across a piece of tin.

'We were just riding through,' Rosalind answered.

The man's attention was transferred to the speaker, as was his rifle. The powder-blackened muzzle was pointed at her like a malevolent eye. Rosalind saw with some surprise the weapon was an old flintlock.

'I don't think we'll get much of a welcome here, Giles,' Celia said. 'These creatures look like they just crawled out from under some rocks and found these houses to live in.'

'Is that so, missus? Just you climb down off them there horses and you'll find out what sort of welcome Jasper Stone has for trespassers.'

While they were talking the silent menacing circle of men closed in around them.

'You have no right to stop us like this,' objected Rosalind. 'I'm sorry we disturbed you. We'll just continue on our way, if you don't mind.'

'Is that so, fella? I have every right to stop anyone as wants to trespass. This here's a toll-road. Every traveller pays us for the use of it.'

Rosalind took a deep breath. 'All right then, how much is the toll?'

The lips parted and blackened, broken teeth were exposed in a bizarre grin. 'Everything. We takes everything

– horses, weapons, money.'

'You robbing son of a bitch!'

Before Rosalind could do anything Celia raised her qirt and swung it at the speaker. With surprising quickness the stocky man ducked the blow and reversing the long rifle drove the butt up into Celia's midriff. So powerful was the blow she was punched out of the saddle. She tumbled backwards over the rear of her horse and landed heavily. Her eyes were wide with pain as she lay in the dirt fighting for breath.

There was a bellow from Henry. He launched his large frame from atop his mount towards the attacker. The two men who stepped in to intercept him were brutally efficient. One rifle smashed into his legs while the other batted him over the top of the head. He went down but was struggling to his feet again when both men raised their rifle butts and smashed them down on his skull. This time when Henry hit the ground he did not stir.

The broken-toothed grin was directed up at Rosalind. 'Young fella, do you need any help gittin' down off that there horse?'

Inwardly trembling with fear and suppressed rage Rosalind dismounted. She ran to Celia. The young girl seemed to be convulsing and was sucking air in long, painful gasps. Rosalind gathered her in her arms and held her close. Rough hands grabbed her and dragged her to her feet.

'Git them all up to the Meetin' House. Drag the big fella and the filly. This young fella can walk on his own feet.'

The men who escorted Rosalind seemed intent on making the walk as difficult as possible. They kicked and punched her all the way. She was unable to see what was happening to her companions. They reached a large wooden structure and she was pushed inside. The insensible Henry was dragged roughly into the building and then the small frame of Celia was tossed callously onto the floor. The door was slammed and in the semi-darkness Rosalind knelt beside her friend. The girl was sobbing piteously.

'Oh, Celia,' Rosalind whispered as she gathered her whimpering friend to her. 'What have I done to bring you to this?'

She looked around the Meeting House. Benches lined the walls and there was some sort of podium at the top of the room. In some ways it reminded her of a primitive church hall.

14

'Jason, have you seen Celia lately?'

Jason, a tall, thin gunman with a drooping moustache, hired as a bodyguard, pursed his lips and thoughtfully shook his head. 'Come to think of it, boss, I ain't seen her for a spell now. She sulking in her room or what?'

'She's not in her room. We had a row and I haven't seen her since. Ask the servants if they know anything?'

Twenty minutes later Jason reported back to Leonard Duke. He had in tow the housekeeper, a chubby Mexican woman.

'No one's seen her, Mr Duke. Maria here seems to think she's gone away.'

Leonard Duke looked up sharply. 'Gone away! What the hell she mean?'

Jason shrugged. 'You better ask her yourself. I can't get much sense out of the fat Mex slut.'

'All right, Jason, leave us. I'll handle this.'

Maria, a short, dark-skinned Mexican, stared malevolently after the tall gunman. She crossed herself and muttered some incantation. 'I not like heem – a peeg.'

'Yeah, yeah, I know, Maria, he's not hired for his social graces but for his skill with a gun. I gotta lot of enemies. Now, do you know where Celia is?'

'Señor Duke, I theenk the *señorita* she go 'way. She take

65

jewels and theengs. Is after that fighting boy was here.'

'The fighting boy! What fighting boy?'

'Señor Sheriff, he want heem. The boy he do boxing. He hurt. Señorita Celia and Señorita Rosalind they repair heem. I find blood on bed. Maria she have to wash. Hard to get blood wash out.'

Leonard Duke was staring hard at the woman. 'You telling me the fella Sheriff Porter was after was here all the time?'

Maria nodded vigorously. '*Sí señor*, he hide in *señorita*'s bedroom.'

'Jason!' Leonard Duke's bellow brought his bodyguard in double-quick time. 'Get Sheriff Porter over here straight away.' Jason touched his hat and left on the errand. 'All right, Maria, that's all for now.'

Jason escorted Sheriff Porter into Duke's study. The sheriff's ruddy face was wet with sweat. It might have been the effort to rush to do his master's bidding or it might have been because of the unease he felt at being summoned so abruptly.

'That goddamn fella you was after the other day – the one as upset the showpeople – you found him yet?'

'No, Mr Duke, he's vanished. My guess is he's fled the county.' The truth was the sheriff had not looked too hard for the youngster. Sheriff Porter liked a quiet life. Chasing elusive youngsters was not something he was keen on.

'Well, find him!' Leonard Duke roared. 'You got a moniker on him?'

Sheriff Porter blanched. 'Sure, boss, he's Owen Lismore. I got his name on the warrant.'

'Lismore! He anything to do with that wastrel as owns the Ayli?'

'Sure, boss.' The fat sheriff nodded eagerly. 'Owen's the younger brother.'

'Then why the hell aren't you out there arresting him?'
Duke was shouting now. It was plain to see from where
Celia had inherited her temper.

'He ain't there. I had a word with his brother, Oliver.
He claims he ain't see his brother since the day of the
fight.'

Leonard Duke was breathing hard as he stared at the
frightened lawman. 'You find Oliver Lismore, Sheriff.'
The words were spaced and even as if Duke was finding it
hard not to reach out and grip the lawman by the throat.
'You will bring him in and lock him up. When you have
him safe you notify me.' Duke sat down and stared at his
desk.

The sheriff stood shifting from foot to foot, unsure of
his next move. Duke suddenly looked up.

'Porter, you any good at emptying spittoons?' The sheriff's mouth hung open. ' 'Cause if you don't get outta here
pronto that's what you'll be doing for the rest of your
miserable life.'

Late that night Leonard Duke walked down to the sheriff's
office flanked by two hard-faced gunmen. The price of
success for the businessman was the undying enmity of
many of the residents of Ayli Valley. As a result he had to
have twenty-four-hour protection.

Sheriff Porter greeted him at the door. Duke swept him
to one side and walked through to the cells. Oliver
Lismore stared sullenly at the newcomer.

'Lismore, where's that brother of yours?' Duke barked
without preliminary.

'How the hell should I know? I've been trying to tell
that fat clown of a sheriff I ain't seen Owen for days. All I
know is he got in some sort of trouble and never came
home.'

Leonard Duke put his hand to his eyes and massaged

his forehead. Slowly he drew his hand down over his face. 'Lismore, my daughter's missing. There's reason to believe your younger brother is in some way involved in her disappearance. He's already in trouble with the law over that bother with the showpeople. When I catch up with him I'll see he gets a long jail sentence for kidnapping.'

For the first time Oliver smiled. 'Well, that's the best news I heard since this thing started. The longer he's put away the better.'

Duke was frowning. 'What the hell's that mean?'

'Mr Duke, I hate my brother. He's the worst trouble-maker I ever come across. I tried my best to keep him straight but he's a wrong 'un. You catch that no-account brother of mine and I'll gladly help you convict him. I'll swear he done all them things you said he's done and more too.'

'You . . . you hate your own brother?'

'Mr Duke, when Pa died I tried to look after the boy. I tried to teach him right. I might as well have spit on a cowchip for all the impression I made on him. He's lazy. Won't do his share of the work around the ranch. He steals what I don't lock away. I tell you, a spell in jail would do him the world of good. He might see the error of his ways.'

Duke stared hard at the man in the cell. 'So you hate your brother. How do you feel like doing a little job for me?'

Oliver shrugged and waited.

'My hunch is this brother of yours is somehow tied in with the disappearance of my daughter. She's friendly with Rosalind Pond. Her father's on the run for cattle-rustling. Somehow this girl, Pond and your brother persuaded my daughter to take all her jewellery and money she had. Then they absconded. You must know where your brother would go. You take a party of my men and find them.'

'I don't particular want to find my brother. If I never see

him again it'll be too soon.'

'You owe a lot of money down at the gaming-tables?'

Oliver looked suddenly wary. 'So!'

'So – I buy them notes. When you bring my daughter back we burn them. As for your brother and that slut, Pond . . .' Duke spread his hands wide like a priest giving benediction. 'I'm not interested in what happens to them.'

The two men stared at each other for a moment. Then Oliver nodded slowly. 'OK, Mr Duke, I reckon as you got yourself a deal. Just one thing, I need Josh Bassinet with me.'

'Just do whatever it takes but don't come back here without Celia.'

15

Owen discovered his new acquaintances lived in a large, dry cave. Primitive though it was, they had made some effort to make it comfortable. They even had bunk-beds and the floor was ankle-deep in fresh straw. Ropes had been slung to keep clothes tidy and lanterns hung from hooks hammered into the walls.

Adam was tucked up in one of the bunks while one of the quartet spooned stew into him.

'I suppose we'd better introduce ourselves. I'm Marvin Pond.' He indicated the man feeding Adam. 'That young fella there is Pete Thomson. The big fella as helped you bring in your friend is Tom Brennon. And that cheery-looking fella with the curly hair is Jack Hallam.'

Owen nodded gratefully at the young man feeding Adam. He was much younger than the rest of the group. He looked to be in his thirties and had a square, pleasant face with a dimple in his chin when he smiled.

'Howdy, fellas, I don't know how we would have fared if I hadn't met up with you. Poor Adam was about finished. I'll never be able to repay you for this.'

'You can repay us by relating your tale of woe as to how you came to be wandering through these dangerous parts, what I believe is full of desperadoes.'

Owen grinned sheepishly at the jibe. 'I sure mistook

you fellas,' he said lamely. 'I'm Owen Lismore and that big fella in the bunk is Adam Jacobson.'

'Lismore. I had a good friend once of that name – Alex Lismore. Owned the Ayli – top end of the valley.'

'You knew Pa! Alex Lismore was my father.'

'Son, you're more than doubly welcome here. Come and sit by the fire and tell us your tale over a coffee.'

They moved to the fire.

'You knew the circumstances of your father's death, Owen?' Marvin Pond suddenly asked as they helped themselves to the coffee.

Owen looked at the man through the steam curling up from his coffee. 'I was told only that he fell off his horse.' He stared wistfully into the fire. 'Everything changed after that. I loved Pa and missed him terribly. After the accident Oliver changed too. He seemed to resent me being on the ranch with him. It was as if he blamed me for Pa's death. Now I realize he hates me. For the life of me I can't think why.

'Your pa was a fine horseman. At the time it looked rather odd that he should fall from his horse. You must know, son, your father was a resolute man. He was organizing the small ranchers to stand up against a man newly arrived in the valley, name of Leonard Duke. They looked up to your pa. With him out of the way resistance crumpled. There was no one to take his place. He was a tower of strength. We all knew something wasn't right when he met with that accident.' He shrugged. 'No one could prove anything. You brother took over the Ayli and sold off bits to Duke. That was the beginning of the end. Duke went from strength to strength and now nothing moves in Ayli Valley without Duke's permission.'

'I knew nothing of this. You saying as my father was murdered?'

'Son, I wish I knew.' Pond shook his head regretfully. 'I

71

wish I knew. Maybe we'll never know now.'

Owen sat digesting all that he had been told. He had just accepted his father's death as an accident and now Marvin Pond was hinting otherwise. The whole business made him feel very sad and very alone.

'Anyway, young 'un,' Tom Brennon interjected. 'You were about to tell us how you wound up here with a bunch of old rustlers.'

So Owen told them about his fight at the boxing tournament and finding Adam, battered and bleeding, lying on the trail on his way back to the Ayli.

'Adam warned me not to go home as my brother Oliver and his sidekick, Josh Bassinet, were fixing to kill me.' Owen looked somewhat embarrassed as he continued. 'I couldn't go back to town as Sheriff Porter had a warrant out for me.'

'Sheriff Porter,' Pond interrupted. 'That's one cunning coyote. Leonard Duke has bought Porter so he can control the law his way.'

'I met this Duke, well I didn't exactly meet him.' Owen tried not to blush as he recalled his unfortunate tangle in the bed with the lovely Rosalind while Celia's father and the sheriff were searching for him. 'I did meet his daughter, Celia and her friend Rosalind.'

'Rosalind? Goddamn it, boy, did you say Rosalind?'

'Yeah, only briefly though,' Owen said defensively, as if the man opposite might know what was troubling him. 'I had to leave in a hurry 'cos the sheriff was after me.'

'Dang my hide, boy, can you describe this here Rosalind? What sort of gal was she?'

Owen gulped. 'She . . . a . . . she was quite tall. And she had auburn hair and green eyes and . . . and . . .' he trailed off at a loss to carry on describing the vision to this stranger.

'That was my Rosalind. I do believe that was my daughter. How was she? Did she seem happy?'

'Your daughter, sir!' Owen gaped at his new friend.

'As I live and breathe that was Rosalind, my only daughter. I had to leave her behind when I fled from Arden Gate. And you're sure she's OK?'

'Yes sir, she was fine.' Owen was desperate to change the subject lest he betray the intense feeling the subject of Rosalind had aroused. 'Why did you abandon your daughter, then?'

Pond stared into the fire before replying. 'Leonard Duke wanted my ranch. I wouldn't sell. He drove some of his steers onto Arden Gate range. Then he had Sheriff Porter arrest me for rustling.' He spat into the flames. 'You probably know what happens to rustlers in this part of the country?'

'They hang them.'

'That's right, Owen. I broke free and ended up here.' He waved his arm round to indicate his companions. 'These fellas were abused in much the same way. Duke had most of my friends killed or run off. Not many had the guts to stand up to him. Now we hide out here in Arden and make raids on Duke's cattle. We drive them through the hills and sell them to a fella in Jordan. He don't pay us much, but,' Pond shrugged, 'then we don't give much for them. It's a miserable life. But it's all we got at the moment. You're welcome to join us. We could sure do with some younger hands. Some of us is getting a mite too old for living this kinda life. Pete Thomson, the young fella as is looking after your injured friend, joined us about a month back. Says as how he knows a bit about medicine. Sure is useful but he don't come much on our raids.'

Owen was quiet while he digested all this. 'It would be an honour to join you, Mr Pond,' he said at last. 'I guess I ain't got many options at the moment. I go back home and my brother has me murdered. I go back to town and

73

the sheriff throws me in jail for winning a boxing-match.'
He sighed deeply.

A vision of a lovely, young girl with auburn hair and
deep-green eyes intruded on his bleak thoughts. He felt a
tingling in his body as he remembered the half-naked girl
stretching out on top of him as he hid in Celia's bed. He
sucked in his breath at the memory and wondered wistfully if he would ever see her again.

16

The Meeting House was a large timber building, more like a barn than an edifice of any significance. Benches were arranged round the walls and at one end a raised platform held a lectern on which a large Bible rested. The walls were covered in writing which on closer inspection were revealed as verses from the Bible. Most were from the Old Testament but the verses ranged from Genesis to Revelation.

Rosalind sat on one of the benches with her arms around Celia. Henry sat nearby staring dully at his hands. The door banged open and the prisoners looked up as people entered. Rosalind had taken to thinking of them as the Flintlock men.

Behind the men and women and children came the brutal Jasper Stone. He walked to the head of the room, stood by the lectern and laid his hands on the large Bible that rested there. He nodded towards the door and two men entered carrying saddle-bags. They slung these on the floor in front of Stone.

The leader of the Flintlocks nodded towards Rosalind and her little party. Rough hands dragged them up and pushed them to stand beside the saddle-bags. Rosalind recognized them as the ones they had brought from Arden Gate. This activity was performed in virtual silence except for the background noise of the people in the hall shuffling their feet and coughing.

'Let us start the proceedings with a prayer.' Jasper Stone bowed his head. 'O come, bless the Divine all you who serve the Divine, who stand in the house of the Divine in the courts of the Meeting House of the Divine. Lift up your hands to the holy place and bless the Divine through the days and nights. May the Divine bless all the souls from Eden. He who made both heaven and earth.'

'Amen,' responded the gathered audience.

Bizarrely, at the end of the invocation Jasper Stone smiled at the prisoners. Rosalind could feel Celia trembling beside her and moved closer to her friend. She stared fascinated at Stone's leering mouth of broken, blackened and missing teeth.

'Welcome to our little community: this is Eden you have landed in. It is fortunate you have fallen in with us for we are a benign people, devoted to the good work of the Divine. We are the Children of Paradise and we welcome you into our community.'

Rosalind could think of nothing to say to this speech. She was numb and full of despair as she stared at this terrible wretch who had so brutally ended their little expedition.

Celia raised her head. 'You are an uncouth brute,' she said, in a voice that was full of repressed anger. 'When our folks find we are missing they'll come into this place and there won't be no place for you to hide. They'll hang you from the nearest tree for daring to molest us.'

Rosalind was relieved that her friend was recovering her spirits but quailed at the sentiments she was expressing. Her tendency would have been to placate these brutes and hope they might allow them to go on their way. Her notion of caution proved to be justified. At a nod from Stone, someone drove a rifle butt into Celia's shoulder-blades. With a sharp cry Celia pitched forward onto the saddle-bags.

'Females are not permitted to speak in the Meeting House,' Stone growled.

Rosalind knelt beside her sobbing friend.

'Get him up on his feet!' snarled Stone.

An arm was wrapped round Rosalind's neck from behind and half-choking she was hauled to her feet. Rosalind glared balefully at the man at the lectern while she massaged her throat. She was sure her neck was dislocated.

'We found the loot from your robbery.' Stone indicated the saddle-bags.

Rosalind found the courage to protest. 'They're not stolen. They are our legitimate property. It is you who steal them from us.'

Stone fixed Rosalind with a baleful eye. 'Three fugitives travelling through Arden with copious riches stuffed into saddle-bags. It is obvious you are fleeing from the law.' He lifted his hand as Rosalind opened her mouth to protest further. 'Don't lie to us, young fella. There's rings and necklaces and gold in them there bags. No honest person would travel with such treasures. So they must be stolen. As marshal and judge in this here community it is my duty to confiscate all stolen property and try to return it to the legitimate owners.

'As for you scurrilous trash, normally we would hang you as we do all thieves. However, I find myself in a benevolent mood today and my decree is that you be allowed to join our community and live in the sanctuary of Eden.'

Rosalind stared aghast at this terrible man so blithely passing judgment on their lives.

'Well, what do you say to my generous offer?'

'Go to hell!' The scream startled Rosalind. Celia was on her hands and knees staring balefully at their self-appointed judge. 'Go to hell you ugly piece of dog shit! You're a liar and a thief and . . .'

Rosalind flung herself in front of the rifle as it swung towards Celia. The blow aimed at Celia's head smashed instead into Rosalind's shoulder. She cried out as the pain lanced through her body. Then she had no more breath to scream. The heavy blows that rained down on her left her writhing in agony and gasping for breath. In vain she rolled away from the rifles being wielded by her guards. She did not witness Henry being beaten into submission by half a dozen of the brutal denizens of Eden. Pain and despair engulfed her and she lay sobbing into the unresponsive wooden floor.

Stone looked impassively at the battered prisoners.

'Take the female to my house. She can cook and clean for me. The big fella can work in the sawpit. That young 'un can work in the fields. But keep an eye on them just in case they might take a notion to run.'

17

They saddled up as dusk approached. There wasn't much talk as they checked girth-straps and bridles. It was a new experience for Owen. He had to make sure nothing on his harness jingled.

'Stealth and quietness is everything,' Pond advised. 'The worst that can happen is the herd will spook. When that happens we usually have to ride back empty-handed.'

'Won't there be a night guard?'

'There always is nowadays. When we first started our raids it was rare to find night-herders. Now Duke posts nightriders almost always. In one way it pleases me he has to pay men to guard against us rustlers. So we hit him both ways. We steal his beef and so he has to pay men to guard them.'

Owen had wrestled with his conscience on the rights and wrongs of stealing cattle. In the end he had voiced his doubts to Pond.

'Son,' Marvin Pond pulled out the makings before continuing. He offered the tobacco to Owen who refused. 'Once upon a time I was an honest cattleman running my own ranch. Then one day Leonard Duke stole that ranch from me. I wanted to strap on my pistol and ride into town and confront the crook. Reason told me that was a foolish move. I knew I wouldn't make it much beyond the boundaries of the town. I would have been shot down like a dog or dragged to the gallows and hanged. So,' Pond lit his roll-up and sucked smoke into his lungs, 'I decided to wage my own little war on my own terms.' He shrugged. 'It's not much, I admit. I'm like a flea on the hide of a coyote. It itches a bit but the coyote can live with that. The coyote scratches at the itch but carries on hunting and scavenging as usual.' Pond looked hard at the youngster. 'You saw what the law does for you in this part of the world. From your own way of telling it, you won that prize-money, fair and square. Yet Sheriff Porter wants to arrest you and slap you in jail. It seems to me, also, that the Ayli belongs as much to you as your brother. Yet he beats your friend half to death and lies in wait to bushwhack you. What you think would happen if you rode into town and told Sheriff Porter you want to lay a charge of assault and intent to murder against your brother?' Marvin Pond blew smoke and stared over Owen's head. 'I ain't telling you to come on this trip. I ain't even asking. One of us has to stay behind and look after your friend, Adam. It might as well be you as Pete.'

The youngest member of the group, Pete, was the self-appointed healer among them. Under his ministrations the big man was making good progress.

In the end Owen had opted to come on the raid. He felt obliged to help on account of the debt he felt he owed the rustlers for rescuing him and Adam. When he told Adam of his decision the man had been dubious.

'One wrong don' make a right, Owen. Stealing is stealing. Dat one of the Bible commands, dou shalt not steal.'

'Goddamn it, Adam, you think I don't know that!' Owen expostulated.

The big hand came out and covered Owen's. 'You take care now, Owen. And remember what I said about swearing. Just mind your language.'

Owen burst out laughing. 'I'm off cattle-rustling and you warn me not to swear at them there ornery steers.' He gripped the big hand in a moment of affection. 'You been a good friend, Adam. I owe you for saving my life. If you hadn't rode out on that road I would have ridden into that bushwhacking brother of mine and his sidekick Bassinet.'

The big man grinned up at Owen as he responded to the youth's sentiments. 'I guess you paid dat debt, Owen, bringing me here. I know dey be rustlers but dey be gut men, anyway.'

They finished their preparations and mounted. Marvin Pond led the way with Tom Brennon following, then Owen and Jack Hallam coming up in the rear. Leaving the rocky hills behind they forded the Estelle and rode for another hour. Owen figured it was well past midnight.

It was eerie riding in silence, with the only noise the faint clip-clop of hoofs when they cantered over rocky ground. There was a tight feeling in his stomach. He had never done anything unlawful in his life and this venture into cattle-rustling left him with many misgivings.

He mused over the strange coincidence of meeting up with Rosalind's father. He wondered if she knew her father was a rustler. Her smiling face was pictured in his mind. There had been a special sparkle in her green eyes as she looked at him. He sighed deeply as he went over the circumstances of their meeting.

She had asked him not to fight John Charles. He knew he couldn't have backed down even to please the beautiful girl who had intruded so abruptly into his life. He groaned inwardly. She must have felt sorry for him, even though she must have looked upon him as a thug.

'Like she would feel sorry for a mangy dog about to be beaten by its master,' he bemoaned softly.

To make matters worse she was forced to lie in bed with him to save him from discovery. In the darkness his face burned with shame at the memory. What a fine, good-natured girl she was to take pity on a stray dog like him.

'Ah, well,' he sighed, 'it's unlikely I'll ever meet her again.'

Which was probably just as well. It would be utterly embarrassing for the girl to have to meet the man who had been so intimate with her young body clad only in her underwear. She had made the sacrifice to conceal him from the law.

'Goddamn it,' he swore silently. His discomfiture grew the more he thought about their meeting. 'Goddamn it!'

But the green mischievous eyes would not go from his mind. So engrossed was he in his uneasy ruminations he almost bumped into the man in front. He reined in when he realized they had halted. The low, gentle sounds of cattle at rest drifted out of the darkness.

'OK, boys, you know what to do. If we have to cut and run we meet up at the ford.'

Owen followed Tom Brennon while their two companions drifted off into the night. His job was to ride around the periphery of the herd and spot any nightriders. To distract them he would stir up the cattle nearest them and then make a run for it as if he had been disturbed at his rustling. The theory was that the nightriders would chase him or Tom, leaving Jack and Marvin free to cut out a bunch of steers and herd them to the ford for the drive back into the hills.

Behind them the night was suddenly rent with yells. A gun went off. Owen realized the roles had been reversed. Marvin and Jack must have stumbled across the night-herders. He heard more shots and looked ahead for his companion. In the dark he could see no one.

'Tom!' he yelled believing the need for silence was now rendered unnecessary.

Somewhere behind him more shots were fired. The

cattle were becoming restless. Owen, not knowing what else to do, did what he knew best. He began to muster the cattle into a bunch.

'Hip, hip!' he yelled and wheeled his pony into a circle. A sizeable bunch of cattle broke away and began to mill aimlessly.

'Hip, hip!'

Pony and rider were one – doing the job they had learned together.

'Whoopee!'

The cattle began to move in the direction Owen wanted. As he worked at the job he knew how to do in darkness or in daylight, Owen forgot these were not his cattle. His pony skipped around the stragglers, keeping good order. The cattle, still drowsy from their disturbed rest, went reluctantly. But the cowboy and his agile pony were more than able to keep them moving. Gradually the hullabaloo that disturbed the night faded into the distance.

For Owen there was just the pleasure of the night-drive. The familiar sounds of cattle protesting – the rumble of hoofs across the ground – the dust and smell of stock on the move – these things were all in his blood.

He arrived at the ford, tired but triumphant, and drove his charges across the river. There he allowed them to rest while he waited for his companions. When they arrived with their haul they would have made a tidy profit on tonight's raid.

18

'You lazy, good-for-nothing slut!'

Jasper Stone swept the dish of food from the table. It clattered onto the dirt floor – the burnt meat and the congealed mess of beans joining the filth already accumulated there. Stone stood up and began the process of removing his belt from around his waist.

'You need a beating, you unclean bitch.'

Knowing what was coming, Celia shrank into a corner. No one who had known Celia in her former life would have recognized the filthy creature cringing in the corner of the dirty shack. Her hair was matted and unwashed. Dark bruises along with congealed blood and dirt almost obscured her face. Her clothes were filthy also. In the few days in captivity she had become indistinguishable from the other miserable females in Eden.

She tried to make herself into as small a ball as possible. The heavy leather belt whooshed through the air and impacted on the girl's arms which she had thrown up to protect her head. She yelled as the leather bit into tender flesh. Her arms were already painfully swollen from previous beatings. The belt rose and fell with monotonous regularity. Celia moaned and cringed. When Stone had first beat her she had tried fighting back. That had only made matters worse. Abandoning the belt Stone had picked up a stout length of firewood and used it to batter her senseless. Now she just cringed and endured and hated. Panting and red-faced at last Stone ceased.

'And clean this place up. It's like a pigsty. Maybe you were used to living in a pigsty before coming here, but in Eden we have certain standards.'

Stone stormed out, locking the door behind him. Celia still crouched in the corner and sobbed. Stone was a brute. She had endured these first days in the hope of escape from this miserable existence. As each day passed hope was slowly fading.

With no means of knowing what had happened to her friends she had made up her mind she would kill herself. She only hoped her friends were in better conditions than was she. In that she was mistaken.

Since their capture Rosalind had been put to work in the fields. Her job was to hoe the rows of melons, beans and whatever sundry crops had been planted. After only one day her hands were raw and bleeding. Blisters had risen quickly on her hands at the unaccustomed work. Even though she had wrapped rags around her skinned hands it made little or no difference.

As she laboured, her guard, a surly man called Seth, would trip her and while she was on the ground he would kick her. Then he would lean on his flintlock weapon and laugh uproariously. His was a perverse and brutal sense of humour.

Every part of her body ached with excruciating, cease-less pain. Bruises erupted on bruises till the simplest move-ment brought agonizing twinges. At night, when she was locked into the Meeting House with Henry, she cried herself to sleep. More often than not she was unable to sleep.

At night Henry would come stumbling in with her and collapse in utter exhaustion and despair, bemoaning the fact there was no news of Celia's fate.

In his distress he sometimes called out her name. Rosalind had to hush the poor youth and remind him constantly of Celia's assumed identity. In the end she had given up. She supposed it mattered little if their true names were revealed now. Their situation seemed hopeless. She could see poor Henry sinking lower with each day that passed.

Henry had been assigned to the sawpit. Normally in this duty the sawyers took turns regarding who would stand in the pit and push and pull the heavy saw from below and who would stand on top. Henry, however, was condemned to the lower position of the labour with no indication that he would ever be assigned to the upper level. Even his giant frame was wilting under the ceaseless effort of the pushing and pulling he was forced to do.

The dust fell in clouds onto his person and coated his hair and lodged in his clothes. It was inevitable he breathed in the dust as he laboured. His coughing kept them both awake during the night. But worse than his own agony was the worry he had for Celia. His despair over her fate was slowly breaking his spirit.

Rosalind tried to give the poor man some hope. But even she was subject to despondency. There seemed no hope from any quarter. No one could know where the were. They had left no clue behind at Arden Gateas to here they were heading. As hope faded so too did the will to live.

Jasper Stone ran his dirty fingers over the glittering pile of jewellery. He had never seen such baubles before and was not sure of their value.

'Them fellas sure made a good haul,' he said to the youngster sitting opposite. The boy was a replica of his father with the same blocky frame and brutal face. 'My guess is they robbed some big house. I bet there would be a substantial reward for the return of these trinkets. But no matter, we just have to use it to our own advantage. Here.' He picked up a green emerald necklace and selected some gold rings. 'In the mornin' I want you to take these to those darn rustlers and exchange them for some beeves. I'm tired of fatback. If they have some good whiskey then get some of that too. That corn-liquor of ours is takin' the skin off my stomach. It's about time we had a feast. We can celebrate the arrival of three new members.' His laugh was harsh and sudden and to anyone not used to it, somewhat frightening. 'Take Sam with you, he'll help you drive back the steers. And mind you get young stuff. Don't take any tough old cows.' Again he laughed harshly. 'I don't want to be reminded of your ma, son. She was tough and she was old and she was ornery.' Pleased with his witticism he laughed again – the sound like a rusty saw-blade biting into an iron nail-head.

19

As Owen peered across the river the dark shadowy figures on the opposite bank resolved into the shapes of men atop horses. He watched anxiously as he tried to make out who was approaching. Self-consciously he loosened the Colt in his holster. Adam had insisted he wear it on the raid.

'Son, we seen some trouble in the last days, I doan want you on dis trip without protection. You doan have to shoot no one,' he added as he saw the reluctance on the youngster's face. 'Just point at the stars and let off a few shots. Den take off as fast as four legs will take you.'

As the riders splashed into the water the hoofs kicked up phosphorescent waves but left the young rustler no wiser as to the identity of the riders. At last he decided to take a chance.

'Hello there, who's that coming across?' he yelled.

Owen sat tensed on his mount, ready to dig his heels in her ribs and flee if the men proved to be unfriendly.

'Howdy, is that Owen?'

Relief flooded through Owen. 'Sure is. I been waiting for you.'

The men came on.

'Where's the cattle?' He suddenly realized the men were not herding any steers.

By now the riders were splashing up onto the bank.

'We ain't got no goddamn steers!' grunted Tom Brennon. 'We were chased off, them bastards getting too smart for us. A whole night wasted.'

The riders were milling round Owen and staring at the dark mass of animals beyond him.

'Where in tarnation did them there cattle come from?'

'I brung them,' Owen answered as the realization began to sink in that he had succeeded where the older hands had failed.

'Well, I'll jump in a bath of beans if the kid ain't gone and rustled us some beeves. Son of a bitch.'

The gang kneed their mounts forward and stared in wonderment at the little herd contentedly waiting on the trail.

'Sumbitch, you didn't just find them here when you rode up?'

'No! I sure as hell didn't!' Owen protested indignantly. 'I cut them out and brung them over here and was waiting for you to join me with your bunch of steers.'

Someone laughed out loud. 'Well, boys, if we ain't got us a ring-tailed, curly wolf here among us. No need for us to ride out on raids any more. We'll just send the Bronco Kid here and he'll bring us all we want.'

Then the horses were crowding round as the rustlers took turns to slap the embarrassed youngster on the back.

'Come on, let's get these little old cows home afore they is missed.'

'Yip, yip, yip! Move them steers outta here.'

Owen rode back slightly euphoric, with his companions' praises ringing in his head.

In a canyon, well removed from their cave, the rustlers had built a corral to contain their stolen cattle. Here, after they changed the brands the rustled steers would be driven to Jordan to be disposed of.

It was a late start for the rustlers next morning. Owen

felt as if he hardly slept at all before the sounds of the camp stirring wakened him. When he emerged from the cave he was pleased to see Adam sitting by the fire, drinking from a mug of coffee.

'Adam, you're up and about. Sure is good to see.'

'Ah, it take more dan a beating to keep dis little ol' Swede down. And how is Bronco Kid dis morning?' Adam grinned widely at his friend.

'Bronco Kid, what's that about?' Owen squatted by the fire and helped himself to a mug of hot coffee. 'Damn me if that coffee ain't the best I ever tasted.'

Pete Thomson yelled from atop the hill where the rustlers kept a look-out from time to time. The two new members of the gang had yet to stand guard but knew it was inevitable if the rustlers decided to let them stay. After Owen's coup last night the issue seemed in little doubt.

'Visitors coming.'

In a short time a couple of strange-looking young men rode into the camp, suspiciously scrutinizing the little group around the fire. Owen eyed them with some curiosity. The youngsters were unkempt with long, greasy hair dangling from under black, high-crowned hats.

'Well, well, well. If it ain't Master Jeremiah Stone and company,' Marvin Pond welcomed the two men courteously. 'Coffee?'

'Yew got nothin' stronger than coffee?' the taller of the pair enquired.

'Sure.' Marvin Pond went into the cave and re-emerged with a bottle of whiskey and two tin mugs. He handed the mugs to the men, uncorked the bottle and poured out generous measures. 'Sorry about the mugs, but we lent out the crystal a few days ago and it ain't been returned yet.'

The two men made no reply but downed the whiskey in a couple of gulps.

'What brings you over this way?' Pond corked the

whiskey and walked back to squat with the others by the fire.

The unkempt pair looked uncertainly into the empty mugs and reluctantly came closer to the fire. Owen noted the rifles the men carried. He was curious to see they were old flintlocks but they looked in good condition. The smaller of the two men was a blunt block of a figure with dark skin and a mean look to his eyes.

'Sit, fellas.' Marvin Pond smiled at his visitors. 'What can we do for you?'

'Pa sent us for some beeves. Gotta be young and tender, though no old cows like Ma was.' The newcomer smiled, pleased he had been able to repeat his pa's witticism.

'Like your ma was – dang me if that ain't a good 'un.' Marvin Pond slapped his knee and guffawed loudly. 'You hear that, fellas? Don't want no old cows like his ma was!'

Jack Hallam and Pete Thomson grinned and made to be mightily amused at the jest.

'How you gonna pay for these young beeves? That last time we traded I wasn't too keen on the scabby vegetables and corn-whiskey you brought us. You'll have to do better this time.'

The youngster smirked. Putting his hand inside his filthy jerkin he produced a rolled-up scrap of material. Carefully he unfolded the bundle and held the contents out for Pond to view.

'Jewellery by Gawd.' Pond massaged his chin as he examined the display. 'Looks mighty pretty. How you boys come by this?'

He got an expressionless shrug for an answer. Suddenly Pond went rather tense and peered keenly at the proffered trinkets. Slowly he reached out a hand. 'May I?'

The thickset fellow nodded, but watched the older man suspiciously. Pond gently extracted a necklace. Green emeralds glittered on a gold chain. Pond held up the item and examined it critically. 'Mmm . . . pretty indeed. Is it valuable?' he asked and Owen thought he noted a slight tremor in his voice.

'Sure is. Gotta be worth a good-sized steer.'

'What else you got?'

'Rings . . . gold rings. Ain't they purty?'

'I'll say they are. How's about a drink to seal the bargain?' Pond slopped more whiskey into the mugs. Eagerly the men downed the fiery liquor. 'Tom, take Jeremiah here to the herd. Let him pick out three good beeves.'

'Three!'

'Sure, three I said. I know a whore in Jordan will entertain me all week for this here necklace alone. We have to blindfold you, Jeremiah,' Pond continued apologetically. 'Can't let you see where we keep our herd. I hear tell there's rustlers in these here hills.'

Everyone laughed deferentially at the joke as they watched Tom Brennon lead the youngster away.

'Now young fella, how about another drink?'

The remaining youngster eagerly held out his mug. 'This here whore in Jordan, what she like? I ain't never been with a whore, ever.'

20

About a dozen men sat or hunkered on the patio of Arden Gate. Three squatted on the steps and played poker for dimes. Others whittled wood or chatted with neighbours. A chuck wagon was parked in the yard. Inside the house the cook kept coffee on the boil and as the day wore on more and more men arrived. They were served with food and coffee. Oliver Lismore interviewed the men as they arrived. Most gave a negative shake of the head.

Outside on the porch Josh Bassinet sat apart from the rest of the men. He stared into the distance with the brooding air of a hunting animal waiting patiently for the quarry to be sighted.

'Ain't no one seen hide nor hair of the pair.' Oliver came and sat beside the gunman. 'Nobody's seen Owen or Celia Duke. You'd think someone would have seen something.'

'Know what I think? They all met up here and headed into Arden. Don't forget what Duke said about Marvin Pond. He reckons he's hiding out in Arden and has been raiding his cattle of a night-time. My guess is the Pond girl persuaded Duke's daughter to go with her. Or likely as not, her and Owen kidnapped the Duke girl and they'll send word to Leonard Duke for a ransom. Find Marvin Pond and you'll find Celia Duke.'

'Dammit, Josh, the more I think of it the more I believe

93

you're right. But how do we find this Pond and his gang? It'd be like looking for a flea on a bear-hide.'

Another rider approached the house. Wearily he swung down.

'Howdy boss, nothing much to report. They had some trouble over on the north side last night. Rustlers made off with a bunch of steers. There was some shooting but nobody hurt.'

Oliver Lismore came of the porch. He quizzed the rider some and then turned to Bassinet who was watching him with a wry smile on his lean, bearded face.

'This is it, Josh – the break we're waiting for. If your surmise is correct, we can track the rustlers and find our quarry.' He smiled slowly as a thought struck him. 'We can kill two birds with one stone. Rescue Duke's daughter and bring in the rustlers.'

The gunman was on his feet. 'Not forgetting we get to even the score with your brother and that Swede of his. Let's go, while the trail is still fresh.'

'Mount up, men,' yelled Oliver. 'We're going after them damn rustlers.'

There was an immediate scramble from the porch and men raced to the corral. For a while all was a hubbub of activity as men roped horses and saddled up.

'The north pastures,' Oliver yelled to the assembled horsemen. 'They crossed the ford there. Let's hope we can follow the trail into Arden.' He grinned suddenly. 'You may get to use your ropes on something more than steers. We might have to stretch a few necks.'

A cheer burst from the horsemen. 'Let's ride!' someone roared. 'We sure know how to stop rustlers from doing their dirty work. Them as we don't shoot we'll hang.'

With excited yells the party flowed out of the yard and headed towards the Estelle and the ford. The quarry was scented and the hounds were hot for blood.

'Tell me more about that there whore in Jordan.' The voice was slurred.

Marvin Pond casually poured another measure into the youngster's mug. He had been filling the youngster's head with fantastical details of the mythical whore of Jordan. As the outlaw leader embellished his tale his listener's eyes grew wider and wider. The youngster slurped the whiskey, never taking his eyes off the speaker.

'When she gets a load of that there necklace she'll not let me outta her bed for at least a week.' The mug was refilled. 'I don't suppose there's any more necklaces where that came from?'

The youngster nodded happily. His eyes were glazed, either from the thoughts of the fabulous whore of Jordan or the whiskey. 'Sure there's more. Ol' Jasper Stone, he took the whole caboodle off them robbers as he collared.'

'Ah, Jasper is lucky the trail runs along that side of the hills. We get no travellers through here. We have to go out and rustle the herds in the Alyi Valley. How many these here robbers were there?'

'Jus' the three.'

The mug was filled again. Owen had lost tally on the amount of whiskey the hill-billy had consumed. He couldn't understand what game Pond was playing, so he waited and watched and said nothing.

'Three big bold robbers, eh. Did they put up much of a fight?'

'Fight – naw, they was easy. Jasper whacked the female off'n the horse. The big fella tried to jump Jasper but Amos and Ezra about bust his skull. The young fella – he came meek and mild.'

'This here female – was she like Mina the whore I'm telling you about, big and busty, or tall and elegant?'

'Naw, she's a skinny little runt. Feisty as a rooster but ol' Jasper he's beatin' that outta her.' The drunken youngster grinned happily. 'We hears her screamin' and it makes us chortle some.'

'What's her name, then?' Marvin asked as he poured more whiskey.

'I reckon theys got them there allyasses. Says as her name is Abigail but the big fella he shouted out Celia a couple of times. They sure some smart robbers them three.'

Owen's ears pricked up. The name Celia and the presence of the 'big fella' were ringing alarm bells in his head.

'The big fella – his name Henry by any chance?' he asked casually.

'Thas right, Henry, you know of these 'uns?'

'I figure they're the Diamond Threesome gang,' Marvin interposed quickly and shot a warning look at Owen. 'Always works in threes – the big fella, Henry, the female is Celia and the young fella as called Jacob.'

'No, no.' Sam was swaying unsteadily while at the same time waving a finger at Pond. 'He's called Giles.'

'Giles, Jacob – maybe I got them mixed up. But they sure sound like the Diamond Threesome, all right.'

The interrogation was interrupted by the return of Tom and young Stone arriving with the steers. The drunken youngster scrambled to his feet and ran to join his companion.

'Maybe I should give these fellas a band to drive them there steers back,' Owen said to Marvin.

Marvin gave him a hard look. 'What's on your mind, kid?'

'Celia is Duke's daughter's name. She had a big fella as worked for her pa, name of Henry. I gotta go see for myself.' He paused. 'You was digging for something yourself?'

96

'That necklace – it might be only coincidence but it was very like one I gave Rosalind's ma.' He grinned mirthlessly. 'That was way back in the days when I was flush. It was made with green emeralds that matched her eyes.' He frowned at Owen. 'You figure as it might be Leonard Duke's daughter held in Eden. All right, kid. You be on your best behaviour. Don't do anything foolish. Deliver the steers and have a look around. But be careful. Them Children of Paradise are a mean bunch. They'd as soon crack your head open as spit in your eye.'

21

'He ain't never had no head for liquor,' Jeremiah Stone said disgustedly.

They had not gone down the trail very far when the drunken Sam had fallen off his pony. With Owen's help, Jeremiah slung him across the saddle and roped the giggling drunk in place. When Eden came into view Sam, in spite of his undignified riding position, was singing drunkenly.

Me an' my wife an' a stump-tailed dog
Crossed Cane River on a hickory log.
The log did break an' she fell in,
Lost my wife an' a bottle of gin.

Owen was mesmerized by the shabbiness of the village of Eden. An air of dereliction, like an infection, overlay the hovels that made up the shanty town.

'Eden,' Owen muttered under his breath, 'looks more like Hell.'

People appeared from the houses and fields to watch the steers being driven in. They were a miserable, hungry-looking tribe. The women were dingy and unkempt. Half-naked, dirty urchins clung to the skirts of the females. The men were gaunt with haunted, suspicious eyes and cruel faces. The sight and sound of Sam brought out laughter and jeers from the onlookers. More than a few were calling out insults.

Grinning broadly, Stone Junior leapt down from his mule, and unloosed the rope holding Sam in place and heaved him unceremoniously to the ground. The drunken youngster fell awkwardly and yelled out a string of noisy curses. Leaving the intoxicated youth where he had fallen, Jeremiah began to herd the steers further into the village.

More and more of the villagers were gathering. They watched as Owen and Jeremiah directed the steers into a pole-built corral. Immediately the crowd surged forward and surrounded the enclosure. They were excitedly pointing and obviously delighted with the beef that had been delivered to the village. The hubbub of voices grew in volume, as did the yells and shrieks of the raggedy children.

Owen slipped down from his pony and quietly led him away. No one took any notice of him as he wandered into the village looking for some sign of the captives who had fallen into the clutches of this wretched community. One clue he had was the sawpit. If the man Sam had told them about was anywhere to be found it would be at the sawpit at this time of day. He spotted the freshly sawn logs and planks strewn about in untidy heaps. With a quickening heartbeat he headed in that direction.

The smell of fresh sawdust hung in the air around the workings. It was a welcome relief from the stale, bitter smell that hung over everything else in the vicinity. Casually he hitched his pony to a fence-post and walked around the site.

Sawdust coated everything. Sawn planks littered the site along with whole tree trunks. Owen surmised the sawyer had some outlet for his products, for there was no sign of building work anywhere in the vicinity. A partly sawn trunk lay over the pit with the handle of the huge crosscut jutting up in the air. Cautiously he looked into the pit. A dust-covered, motionless figure crouched in the pit.

'Henry?'

The dust shifted and a head was upraised. Owen did not know who or what lay beneath the coating of sawdust. The man raised a hand and shaded his eyes.

'What you want?'

'Henry, is it really you? It's Owen Lismore.' Owen lay full length on the ground and peered into the pit.

The sawdust creature continued to stare up at Owen without recognition.

'Remember the fella you rescued from the boxing and brung back to Miss Celia's house?'

Recognition flickered in the dull eyes. 'Yeah, I remember. What's happened to Miss Celia?'

'I was hoping you could tell me that.' Owen looked at the big chap now standing upright in the pit. 'How do you get in and out of there?'

'There should be a ladder.'

Owen looked around and spotted a crude ladder of untrimmed branches. Quickly he hauled the piece over and lowered it into the hole. Henry reached up to assist in positioning it. Owen held the ends of the ladder.

'Come on, Henry, we'll find Miss Celia together.'

Too late he saw Henry's eyes widen as the man looked past him. He tried to turn to see what had alarmed Henry. The top of his head drove in with such massive force that Owen pitched into blackness.

Henry, standing with one foot on the bottom rung, broke his fall.

Someone was calling to him from a long way away. At the same time someone else was banging on his head with a blunt axe. He was curious as to who it was calling him, but much more he wanted the one with the blunt axe to stop hammering it on his skull. When at last he was able to open his eyes a face was hovering over him.

'Am I dead?' he managed to croak.

'Owen, thank God you've come round.'

The fuzziness in his vision cleared slightly while the pain in his head intensified. A very dirty youth was bending over him.

'Owen, I knew you'd come for me. I'm so sorry!'

Owen looked in puzzlement at the youth. The face was encrusted with dirt. Twin channels wound down his cheeks where tears had washed away some of the dirt. Yet there was something vaguely familiar about the youth. Owen felt extremely embarrassed. Roughly he pushed the youth from him. The effort intensified the pain in his skull.

'Goddamn it, I didn't come for you. I came for Miss Celia. Now stop fussing over me. I can't stand cry-babies.'

The youth looked shocked and then his mouth tightened. 'Very well, then, and how is that a way to repay a girl that rescued you from a boxing swindle.'

Gingerly Owen explored the top of his head. His fingers found a large, tender lump. 'I said I come to rescue Celia. What more do you want?'

'What about her friend, the one as risked her good name by lying in bed with you.'

Owen gaped. The youth suddenly smiled at him.

'I'm Rosalind's twin brother. I thought you'd recognize me straight away.'

Owen peered at the youth. He looked hard at the dirt and the hacked-off hair, then gazed into the eyes. Mischievous green eyes stared back at him.

'Rosalind, that blow on the head must have addled my brain. Am I mad or is it really you?'

'I'm afraid so. Much as I'm glad to see you I would far rather it were under better circumstances.'

'Rosalind,' Owen said faintly. 'I'll be blowed, you and Celia and Henry. How come you're all here in this hell-hole.'

Before she could reply a movement to the side caught his attention. Henry sat morosely watching him.

'That Jasper Stone came up behind you and hit you with a log. I couldn't do nothing. You fell on top of me.'

'Jasper Stone? Is he the leader of this nest of rats?'

'Yes,' Rosalind answered, 'he's a vicious thug – mean and brutal.'

Slowly Owen got to his feet. A wave of dizziness threatened to overwhelm him. He gritted his teeth and stared around the large room. 'What's this place?'

'They call it the Meeting House. It's like a kind of church to them.'

A dim light filtered down from a couple of skylights in the roof. The few windows in the wooden walls were shuttered from outside.

'What happens when they come to fetch you or feed you?' he asked. He was staring at Rosalind. He still could not believe he was here with the girl who had occupied so much of his thoughts since that first meeting at the boxing.

'There's always two of them with the food. One stands in the doorway with a gun while a female carries the food into us. We get nothing but grits or stale bread. When they want us for work the one in charge of the fieldwork takes us out. He drops Henry off at the sawpit and then takes me down to the fields. He's as mean as the rest of them and he's always armed.'

Owen felt confident enough to take a few steps. The room swayed dangerously but he managed to stay upright.

'When are they next due?'

The girl shrugged expressively. 'I don't know. We were brought in early. There was a lot of excitement. Someone delivered some steers and they all want to be in at the butchering.'

Owen nodded thoughtfully – or at least started to nod. He stopped abruptly as the pounding in his head intensified. As he surveyed the room in an attempt to seek a means of escape the only thing that stood out from the rest of the décor was the lectern. This was made of a stout post with a flat board nailed to the top to take a book. He looked at Henry sitting despondently on one of the benches.

'Give me a hand, Henry to see if we can't loosen that post. We just might be able to use it as a weapon.'

He walked to the top of the room, every step producing a sharp throbbing in his skull. Behind him he heard the dull steps of Henry as the man followed him.

From outside came shouts and screams mingled with loud bellowing from the steers. Owen paused to listen. The butchery of the steers was getting under way.

22

The steers were bellowing in terror now. More and more villagers gathered round the corral. There was an air of festivity. The arrival of so much prime meat into their midst brought nervous animation into the brutal life of these degenerate people. They craved the fresh blood and the flesh of these meat-rich animals. Already they were salivating at the thought of the juicy steaks roasting over their fires.

The hides would be used to fashion many useful items. The fat would be used in cooking. Even the bones would be ground down and fed to the hogs. But more important was the blood that would pour from the butchered animals – blood that could be used to make many tasty delicacies.

There were those amongst the onlookers who craved the blood raw. The warm salty liquor was the stuff of life. They gathered around the beasts and cried out in hungry anticipation.

Jasper Stone stepped forward. He was the high priest. To him fell the duty of conducting the sacrifice.

'Get some of those there poles. We need to make a tripod.'

Many eager hands rushed to do his bidding. The posts were quickly erected and the tops bound together with rawhide. A loop hung down from just below the apex.

'Get one of the beasts over here.'

Inside the enclosure the steers plunged and bellowed in terror. No one dare get in among the lunging animals. Several men attempted to rope the beasts while standing on the rungs of the corral. While the crowd watched enthralled, encouragement and advice came from every direction.

'Rope the hind leg, Jeremiah!'

'Get a rope on the horns!'

'You couldn't rope a chimney!'

'Someone'll have to git in there and hold the dad-blamed beasts afore there's any ropin' done.'

Eventually the ropes entangled one of the steers by the head and a hind leg. Bellowing loudly it was dragged towards the gate. In spite of the beast's superior strength, with the many hands hauling in the ropes the animal was forced foot by foot across the corral. Amidst mounting excitement the bars were dropped, the steer was out and its doom was now inevitable.

People were crowding round, forcing the animal towards the makeshift tripod. A skinny man with dirty blond hair, holding a crude hook, danced excitedly around the rump of the steer.

'Get a rope on the legs, goddamn it.'

A loop was spread on the ground and the animal was pulled and tormented till its feet landed inside the noose. With whoops of delight the rope was pulled tight. The animal felt the rope and tried to buck. As it did so more ropes landed on the horns and head. Another noose was snaked onto the front legs. A roar of triumph erupted as the beast toppled over with an earth-shaking thump. The man with the hook darted in. He drove the hook into the fleshy part of the hind leg. The animal thrashed round on

105

the earth, churning up the soil. Pain as well as fear was now mingled in its bellowing.

A rope was quickly fastened to the hook and this was swiftly taken to the tripod. The animal struggled wildly but inexorably it was being dragged to the place of execution. The rope attached to the hook was taken through the loop at the apex of the tripod. There were many willing hands to haul on the various ropes attached to the animal's limbs and head. Slowly the terrified animal was hauled beneath the tripod. The iron hook embedded in its leg rose in the air and the bellowing steer was inched upwards. At this stage of the affair there was mad cheering from the assembly. It was time for the butchery to begin.

Owen threw himself against the lectern once again. The wooden stand groaned as the upright leaned forward. In a sudden frenzy of energy Henry strained backwards, his huge hands wrapped around the flat bookrest. Before they started Owen had removed the large Bible, laying it reverently on the stage. Then he had attacked the lectern itself.

Every effort sent waves of pain surging through his head. He felt the dizziness sweep over him but refused to give up.

'Damn you, give!' he said through gritted teeth.

Rosalind suddenly threw her weight behind that of Owen and with a creaking, rending groan the lectern gave way. Henry staggered back, fighting to keep his balance. But it was a losing battle. His feet went from under him and he lay gasping on his back like a winded steer, the wooden stanchion still clutched in his big hands. But for the seriousness of their situation Owen would have burst out laughing. The pain in his head prevented any levity.

'At least we've got a weapon,' he panted instead.

They moved to the door with Henry carrying the broken stand. Owen paused and listened. The noise of festivity, if anything, was becoming even more uninhibited. Owen shivered. The roaring and screaming from the villagers was almost bestial.

'Sounds as if the party is really getting under way.' He paused as a thought occurred to him. 'If them there savages are so busy out there it might be our chance to make a break for it instead of waiting for them to come to us.'

His original idea had been to clobber the guard with the heavy piece of wood they had recovered from the broken lectern, but now his thoughts took another turn. He studied the door.

The hinges were made of stout wooden brackets. A space between door and hinge gaped invitingly. Owen took the wooden stand from Henry and inserted the flat portion of the stand into the gap.

'While I hold this in position you pull down on the post.'

Henry obediently gripped the thick upright and began to exert pressure on the structure. Except for a faint creaking of wood everything remained firm.

While these operations were going on Owen had tried to ignore Rosalind. That had been hard to do for she been exceedingly solicitous for his welfare. Now she hovered uncertainly while the two men worked at demolishing the stand. While Owen held the lever in position, Rosalind reached forward and added her weight to that of Henry. Owen smiled encouragement to her.

For moments nothing could be heard inside the Meeting House but the creaking of the timber as the trio levered at the hinge. Owen could do little to help for he was engaged in keeping the bookrest wedged underneath the hinge. He was about to ask Rosalind to change places with him so he could add his considerable strength to that of Henry when there was a slight give in the lever.

'Harder,' he yelled. 'Pull harder!' He wished he hadn't spoken so forcefully for his head vibrated painfully with the effort.

Stut-stut-stut-stut . . . the lever visibly moved and the wooden hinge began to shudder under the strain. He had just turned to encourage his helpers when above his head the hinge burst asunder.

'Goddamn it, we've done it!' he exulted. 'We've done it!' Then he paused and listened. The frenzied noise from the denizens of Eden had not abated. So far the noise of their own efforts seemed to have gone undetected.

While his companions waited patiently Owen once again examined the door. With the hinge ripped from its moorings a gap had appeared at the top of the door. Daylight could now be seen between the wood of the frame and the door.

'Come on.' He grabbed the broken lectern from Henry and jammed it into the gap. With Henry by his side they heaved mightily on the makeshift lever. The door groaned and Owen could feel the wooden shaft quiver under his hand as wood was forced against wood.

'Come on, you bitch,' he grunted.

Though there was not room for all three, nevertheless Rosalind pushed in between the two straining men and added her efforts to theirs. There was something very distracting about the girl pressed so intimately against him. For now, all Owen could do was smile encouragingly at her and force his muscles to even greater efforts. The door gave without warning.

One moment the trio were jammed together in a sweating mass, then there was a loud rending noise. Then everything gave way and the door crashed in on them. They fell to the floor with the door and lever on top of them. For a moment all was confusion, then they were scrambling from beneath the broken door. Bruised, breathless but triumphant, they peered out at daylight and freedom.

23

The twitching steer hung head down, its neck gaping open from a fearsome gash. Jasper Stone watched with glazed eyes as the animal's blood spurted from the wound. A large zinc bath stood beneath the dying beast. The blood had almost filled the container. The inhabitants of Eden were crowding round, dipping mugs in the bath and slurping greedily at the hot liquor. Some even dipped cupped hands in the blood and with evident pleasure licked the crimson gore from grubby paws. Jasper looked down at the bloody knife in his hand. As leader of the village it had been his task to make the sacrificial cut.

The knife stood proud and erect in his fist with the bright blood dripping slowly from the honed steel. For a moment he stared at the knife. Killing the steer had fulfilled a need in his bestial soul, but now another need surfaced. His mind focused on the young woman he held captive in his cabin.

She was feisty but he was beating her into submission. Suddenly he knew the time was ripe for her complete subjugation. While his fellow citizens were engaged with the feasting he would initiate the female into the final act of submission. The lust was growing in him in an irre-sistible inflammation of desire. He turned from the dying steer and the men waiting with the sharp knives to begin the butchering and slipped away. No one noticed him go.

As the three fugitives crept forward they realized the noise of the escape had gone unheard by the mob down in the village. Owen carried the broken lectern with him as a makeshift weapon. They bypassed the sawpit.

'Wait,' Henry hissed. He tramped over to the heaps of timber and reappeared almost immediately, carrying a long-handled axe.

Owen nodded approvingly. They had just begun to go forward when all three halted again. A low mumbling came from somewhere ahead. Cautiously they crept forward.

'Me an' my wife an' a stump-tailed dog . . .'

Propped against a water butt was Sam, singing quietly to himself. In his hand he gripped a partly full bottle. Owen stepped forward.

'Howdy, Sam. You look as if you're having a good time.'

'Come on in.' Sam waved a drunken welcome. 'Everyone's gone to hell or somewheres.' He peered intently at Owen. 'You bin with that there whore that fella was tellin' us about?'

'No, I never did have that pleasure.'

'Damn shame. You wanna drink?'

'Sure.' Owen took the proffered bottle. Carefully he sat it on the cover of the water butt. He squatted before the bemused youth. 'I'm sorry about this, Sam. You seem a decent sort of fella.'

The uppercut was one of Owen's best. It travelled only a short distance but connected with the point of Sam's chin with sufficient force to bounce the youth's head against the water-butt. His eyes glazed over and he slid to one side. Owen searched the youth and found a powder-horn and a bag of lead balls. When he rose to his feet he gathered up the flintlock lying in the dirt nearby.

'It ain't much but now we got an axe and a rifle.' He grinned without mirth at his companions. 'We just find Celia and then get the hell out of here.' Before they moved on he noticed the haft of a Bowie in the belt of his victim. Quickly he plucked forth the weapon and handed it to Rosalind, standing beside Henry. 'Just so's you don't feel outta things.'

The scream when it came sounded close. It startled them sufficiently for all three to stop and look towards the sound.

'Celia,' gasped Rosalind.

Owen stared at her. 'You sure?'

She nodded emphatically, a frightened look in her eyes. There was another scream. Henry rushed towards the sound, his axe balanced over his shoulder, to all appearances a lumberjack hastening to his work.

'Wait,' Owen hissed but Henry either did not hear him or was ignoring him. Owen was forced to hurry after him.

Henry had homed in on the cabin from where the screams were coming. The door was slightly ajar and Henry blundered through just as a man's voice rose in anger.

'You bitch! You do what I tell you.'

There was a sudden wild scream and the scuffling of boots on a wooden floor. Then Henry emerged from doorway he had just entered. A thickset, muscular man was savagely pummelling the big youth. Kicking, punching, and swearing – the very ferociousness of the onslaught was driving the big fellow back out into the daylight. In the mêlée, Henry's axe fell to the ground as he tried to counter the frantic assault. He was punching and slapping his attacker but he might as well have been trying to stop a crazed wildcat.

Jasper Stone was an instinctive fighter and killer. He was

112

a wild animal disturbed in its den. His reaction was to go berserk. He could not be stopped now. He drove his fists into Henry with the force of a steam-hammer. Henry, a big soft man and weakened by his brutal time in the sawpit, gave way before the frenzied attack.

Henry was not a fighter. He was a large, strong youth but totally inexperienced in the craft of fighting. Jasper Stone was literally beating him to a pulp. In the short time the assault had taken Henry's nose had started bleeding. His eye was split. Blood poured from his crushed nose and lips. He fought bravely but ineffectually against the madman.

A slim figure dashed past Owen and he saw Rosalind dart in through the open door of the cabin. Jasper Stone, realizng he had more than one person up against him, reacted like the wild animal he was akin to. His one thought was to dispose of his opponent and retreat back to his den. Swiftly he gripped the injured Henry and crashed his head against the young man's face. Such was the force of that blow that Henry went down like a pole-axed bear.

Belatedly Owen brought the stolen flintlock to bear and pulled the trigger. There was a loud metallic click. For some reason the gun misfired. Before he could check the weapon a whirlwind of bone and gristle plunged into him.

Owen staggered back and went down under the onslaught. Stone gripped the weapon and wrenched it from his grasp. Owen saw the rifle rise in the air as Stone prepared to smash the butt into his face. Desperately he rolled. The rifle butt crashed into his shoulder. He felt an agonizing pain lance down his body. Trying to ignore the hurt he lashed out with his boot, aiming for Stone's crotch. Stone howled then. It was a sound that chilled Owen – a primal cry of a mortally wounded animal.

Stone's face was working spasmodically. Owen was wriggling back to get away from the man, not knowing what was happening. Then he saw Henry. He was tugging the axe from where it was embedded in Stone's back. There was blood on the axe-head. Henry raised the axe above his head. The axe swept down again and struck Stone in the back of the head. He pitched forward onto Owen.

The youth wrestled desperately with the convulsing body of Stone. Horrible gulping sounds came from the open mouth and blood sprayed onto Owen. Owen could not help himself as he screamed – desperately punching and kicking the dying man away from him. Stone gave one or two last twitches and then lay still – a gaping wound in the back of his head and another in his lower back. Owen looked at Henry. His companion was gazing in horror at his handiwork. He dropped the bloodied axe, fell to his knees and began to heave.

24

Owen picked himself up and stumbled past the bent-over Henry to the door of the cabin. As he pushed inside he could make out no details, for the interior was very dim. To make sure his prisoner could not escape Stone had closed and secured the heavy wooden shutters. The only light now filtered in from the doorway. As he stepped inside a flash and a movement warned him. With a quickness learned from his boxing practice he reacted swiftly. Twisting sideways he lashed out with his fist. There was a startled grunt as he connected with something solid. He caught a glimpse of a body falling to the floor.

'Goddamn it!' he swore and knelt beside the body.

Rosalind lay sprawled across the floor. Owen had a momentary inclination to flee before the girl recovered and found out who had hit her. On the floor lay the knife that had been intended for him. A movement at the further side of the room caught his attention. He prepared for another challenge when he paused. As far as he could tell in the dim light he was facing a young woman. The small figure was poised in a corner – a large frying-pan raised above her head. Owen stared at the dishevelled figure. Something about her was familiar.

'Miss Celia, is that you?'

Her face was dirty. Hair that he had last seen tied back

in a tight bun hung in untidy disarray and, worst of all, her dress was ripped to shreds. Owen could not help but stare at the small perfectly shaped breasts now exposed where the fabric had been ripped away. Slowly she lowered the pan.

'Owen, Owen Lismore . . .'

'Sure, miss. We got to get out of here. Henry's outside . . . he . . . he finished off Stone.'

'The beast attacked me,' the girl said softly. 'But I fought him off.'

'Yes, miss.' With an effort Owen averted his gaze from the semi-nude figure. 'Can you find something to wear?' he continued awkwardly. 'Your clothes are all torn. I'll be just outside.'

A groan from the floor drew his attention. He shook his head in frustration at not recognizing Rosalind before punching her. Bending down he gently touched her face.

'Rosalind, I'm sorry. I didn't know it was you.'

'Oooh . . .'

Owen squirmed as he listened to the groans of the girl. He picked her up and carried her outside.

'Henry?'

Henry was standing upright but swaying unsteadily – his face was whey-coloured beneath the grime and sawdust.

'I'm OK.'

Owen glanced dubiously at the youth but made no further comment.

'Miss Celia's inside, she seems all right. Miss Rosalind got a bump but I've got her safe now. We got to make tracks before those savages discover we've gone.' He considered whether to pick up the discarded flintlock lying by the bloodied corpse of Stone. Then decided it might be of some use as a club rather than as a firing-piece.

'Grab that axe,' he called to Henry. 'It might come in

116

handy if we're attacked again.'

Henry backed away. 'I ain't touching that there axe no ways.'

Owen sighed. Rosalind stirred in his arms. She opened her eyes. 'Owen, what happened?'

Owen winced when he saw the swelling on the girl's jaw. He considered lying to her, but holding her close like this stirred him to tell the truth. 'Rosalind, I'm sorry. I thought you were someone else. It was dark in the cabin.' He trailed off lamely.

Rosalind stared up at him with those disturbing green eyes.

'I think I was trying to stab you. I thought you were Stone coming in after me.'

For a long disturbing moment they stared into each other's eyes. Before either could say anything Celia appeared in the cabin doorway.

'Oh, Rosalind.'

The girl wriggled out of Owen's grasp and the two girls tearfully embraced. Owen looked on, feeling somewhat pleased that he had played a major part in reuniting these two friends.

Celia had found a man's shirt and pulled that over her ruined clothing. The shirt draped her slight figure like a dress, falling to just above her knees. She was wearing a pair of men's drawers, which were also oversize, and now she looked like nothing more than a ragged urchin.

'Come on,' Owen intervened. 'Any minute now these denizens of hell will be about our necks.'

He led the way back towards the sawpit. On the way to rescue Celia he had noticed his pony still tethered where he had left it. Having recovered the pony, the refugees crept from the village. The sounds of the feasting faded as they filed down the trail with Owen leading. No one spoke – each sunk in their own misery.

117

Well, at least I rescued Duke's daughter, Owen mused as they progressed. And wondered how grateful the man would be. According to Pond, Leonard Duke was a ruthless business baron who arranged for people to be killed or frightened off when he wanted their property. Pond's surmising regarding the circumstances of the death of Owen's father had been disconcerting to say the least. If his father had been organizing resistance to Leonard Duke's expansion plans then it made sense for Duke to have him killed.

It was a gruesome thought for Owen. He did not know enough about Duke to form an independent opinion of the man. Other than hearing his voice when Duke and Sheriff Porter had barged into Celia's bedroom searching for him, Owen had never met the man.

Yet if he was a murderer and a swindler his daughter was the opposite. She had schemed with Rosalind, at some risk to herself and her own good name, to rescue him from the boxing marquee. Still, he hoped he had now repaid the debt by taking the girls and Henry from the clutches of the Children of Paradise.

As they walked, Owen now had time to take stock of his own condition. The blow on his head at the sawpit was stll painful. In the course of Stone's savage attack the clan leader had battered him unmercifully. His shoulder ached considerably where Stone had hit him with the flintlock.

'I feel as if I just done ten rounds with that John Charles,' he muttered.

He gazed ahead at the trail and then glanced back at the ragged trio following behind. They stumbled along, putting one foot in front of the other, weary with exhaustion.

At least Rosalind was now safe, he mused. The thought of the tall, willowy girl brought a warm glow and momentarily took his mind off his aches and pains.

Once they were well away from the village Owen stopped and faced the girls. They looked expectantly at him.

'Well, I got some good news at least, for you Rosalind. I fell in with your pa, Marvin Pond. It was him as recognized your necklace that Stone junior brought to trade with. He'll be real glad to see his daughter again.'

Rosalind put both hands to her mouth.

'Owen, that's wonderful. We were on our way to find Pa when those brutes took us prisoner. Is it far?'

'It's a fair piece. If you and Celia want to ride you can both sit atop my pony. I'm sure she won't mind the double weight, seeing as we'll be going at walking-pace.'

Their progress was slow. With the two girls clinging to the back of Owen's mount, they trudged wearily along – the trail stretching interminably long and rocky before them.

After what seemed hours later, as the light was just beginning to dim, he smelt the wood-smoke and realized they were at journey's end.

'Almost there,' he called out. He looked behind him at his dirty and dishevelled companions. Rosalind gave him a wan smile. Owen smiled back. It felt good to be in her company no matter the circumstances. He was almost staggering with weariness and he felt all he wanted was a bed and a soft pillow and he would sleep for a week.

He spotted the figures sitting around and, as was customary when approaching a campsite, he called out a greeting.

'Howdy, fellas, I brung some guests back for supper.'

Heads lifted up and men rose to stand, watching the little party as they tramped nearer.

'Well, well, well. If it ain't my own long lost little brother.'

25

'Oliver!'

Bewildered by the unexpected appearance of his brother at the rustlers' hideout Owen stopped abruptly. His travelling companions caught up with him. The two girls slid from the pony and stood beside him, shoulders drooping dejectedly. Owen's eyes shifted to the men with his brother.

Bassinet was there – watching him from his hostile, slate-grey eyes. Owen did not recognize the other hard-cases with his brother. A cold feeling gripped his insides.

'What are you doing here?' Owen asked shakily.

Oliver did not answer. There was movement to either side of the group and men emerged from the cover of the rocks. Like the ones at the camp-fire they were hard-eyed and every man was armed.

'Look at what he's brought in – a bunch of saddle tramps,' sneered Bassinet.

'Yeah,' agreed Oliver, 'you're a disgrace to the family name. You wreck a boxing-booth and try to kill the people as run it and Sheriff Porter has a warrant out for your arrest and then you take up with rustlers and saddle tramps. I ought to trash you good.'

'What you done with Pond?' Owen gritted. He heard a sharp intake of breath from Rosalind.

Before Oliver could reply Bassinet interjected; 'What does one do with a bunch of low-down, stinking outlaws? We've roped them all together back in the cave.' He flicked his thumb towards the cave mouth. 'They're all trussed up safe and sound along with your Swede friend. We haven't decided yet whether to shoot them or hang them. We were waiting for you to show up so you could join your outlaw associates.'

Before Owen could reply, Celia stepped forward. She was a sorry sight with her dirty face and unkempt hair and dressed in a shirt that was about four sizes too big for her.

'Howard, what are you doing here?' she called.

One of the men by the fire frowned and peered hard at the filthy waif who had addressed him. He was a big rangy man with wide shoulders and a dark moustache. 'Who the . . . what the. . . !' He was plainly at a loss.

'Jackass!' Celia's fiery spirit was beginning to reassert itself. 'I'm Celia Duke. I'm a bit knocked about because I was kidnapped by a bunch of hill-billies. This fella,' Celia jerked her thumb at Owen, 'rescued me and brought me back here. Now what the hell's going on?'

'Miss Celia, I sure didn't recognize you in that there get-up. Your pa sent us out to find you. He figured this Lismore fella kidnapped you. He hired his brother Oliver and Bassinet to take a party of us out and search for you. He'll sure be pleased to find you safe again.'

'Well, you've found me, or rather Owen found me,' snapped Celia. 'Now get us some food. We're starved and tired.' She moved forward towards the fire.

'Sure, miss . . . I . . . I . . .' The big fellow was at a loss. He looked uncertainly at Oliver and Bassinet.

Oliver nodded. 'Look after her, but you lot stay put.' He indicated Owen and his two remaining companions.

Celia stopped moving forward. 'I said, we needed food. And that means me and these people too.' Her eyes were flashing fire again. Stone's brutal treatment had not extinguished her spikiness. Her voice raised a pitch. 'Seeing as my father hired you, then you're under my orders now.' She glared at Oliver and Bassinet.

'Sorry, Miss Celia,' Bassinet drawled. 'You see, we hired out to your father. It means we don't take no orders from no female. You may be Celia Duke but we're here to rescue you and take you back safely to your pa. We don't help nobody else and especially those that is wanted by the law.'

'What the hell do you mean, taking that tone with me?' Celia said coldly. 'Howard, see him to his horse. You, mister, whoever you are, can go on your way. I don't need protection from the likes of you.'

Bassinet laughed. He allowed his hand to drop casually to his side. 'Howard, why don't you do as your mistress asks?'

The challenge was unmistakable. Howard was a big man – his shoulders broader than the average. He was no coward but he knew he was no match for the gunslinger if it came to a gunfight.

'I know you can beat me to the draw, Bassinet. I ain't foolish enough to commit suicide. Begging your pardon, Miss Celia, it's more than my life's worth to try and do what you said. I'm sorry, miss.'

'He's right,' interrupted Owen, 'Bassinet's a cold-blooded killer. He'll shoot Howard with the same feeling as he'd step on a bug.'

The gunman's cold eye fastened on Owen. 'I've got your Swede friend inside, Owen. Had to pistol-whip him some to pay him back for that time he hit me back at the Ayli. Had to get some men to hold him while I bust his face up some.'

Owen hurled himself towards the gunman. He could not help himself A bitter rage at Bassinet's cruel jibe regarding Adam overrode all caution.

As he moved, he raised the flintlock with the intention of clubbing the gunman to the ground. Owen did not see the boot his brother thrust out as he lurched towards Bassinet. Nor did he see the pistol appear suddenly in Bassinet's hand. As he went down he heard the roar of a shot and the flash of a pistol going off almost in his face. Something struck him a stunning blow on his temple. Owen went down and did not move again.

For a few seconds there was a stunned silence as the spectators stared at the man on the ground. Blood spilled slowly from the dark wound in the youngster's head. With an anguished cry, Rosalind flung herself forward onto Owen's inert body.

Oliver was staring at his brother with a stricken look. 'Goddamn it, Josh! Did you have to shoot him?'

'What the hell! You expect I should stand still and let him bludgeon me to death with that?' Glaring at Oliver, Bassinet nudged the fallen flintlock with his boot. 'Where the hell he came upon that antique?'

'Yeah, but . . .'

Bassinet ignored Oliver. 'Get over by the fire with the others.' He snarled and kicked Rosalind in the side of the head.

Rosalind sprawled on her back. 'He was right.' The girl shot a look of pure hatred at the gunman. 'You're nothing but a cold-blooded killer.'

Ignoring her venom, Bassinet herded her and Henry towards the central fire. Owen's body lay where it had fallen – a pool of crimson spreading out from the ugly wound in the youngster's head.

26

Over by the camp-fire the three friends crouched together, cowed by the sudden violence to one of their company. Henry hovered close to Celia and Rosalind. Celia tried once more to remonstrate with Bassinet but she might as well have addressed the rocks that bordered the campsite.

'What'll do we do now?' Oliver asked his companion.

The gunman was relishing the power his prowess with the six-gun had brought him. Duke's men had been ordered to assist Oliver and Bassinet, so they had to defer to the two men who headed the expedition to find Celia Duke. The mission had been successful. They had found the boss's daughter. Not only that but they had also captured the rustlers who had plagued Duke's herds.

Bassinet cast his eye around the barren rocks. The place had been an ideal hideout for the outlaws. The cave in the rockface had given them shelter from inclement weather. A rock-fall at some time in the past had formed a natural barrier behind which they could shelter and build cook-fires with little fear of being detected.

The rustlers' normal vigilance had slackened as their leader had pondered the significance of the necklace offered as payment for the stolen beeves. He had also been concerned about the safety of the youngster who had volunteered to ride to Eden in order to spy out the activities there and identify the captives Sam had boasted about.

Bassinet had spotted the smoke from the camp. Leaving the horses he had led Duke's men right up to the rustlers' hideout without being detected. With such a large party of gunmen surrounding them the rustlers had no option but to throw up their hands in defeat.

Finding Adam had been a bonus for Bassinet. No one in his party had had the temerity to interfere as the gunman pistol-whipped the big Swede after he had been hogtied.

'We should be heading back now,' Oliver suggested. 'Duke is sure to reward us for the good work we done here. We got his daughter back and rounded up the rustlers. We'll be in his good books for sure.'

Bassinet smiled cynically at his companion. 'Not so fast, Oliver, don't be in such a dad-blasted hurry to get away from here. There's unfinished business to take care of.'

'What you mean?' Oliver asked uneasily. 'We done everything.'

'There's still the matter of that there Swede. He still has to pay for that hiding he gave me back at the ranch.'

Oliver eyed his friend anxiously. 'What you talking about? You already beat him half to death.'

'He's a big man, Oliver, used to fighting with his hands. I aim to give him a chance to prove himself with a gun.'

'Josh, there's been enough bloodletting. Let's just mount up and take them back to town. Let Sheriff Porter deal with them.'

Josh laughed out loud. 'You feeling sorry about that no-account brother of yours? Your conscience bothering you? Let me just remind you who lay in wait back at Ayli prepared to bushwhack the son of a bitch?' For a moment he glared at Oliver. The rancher dropped his eyes. Bassinet smiled cynically and then turned abruptly. 'You, throw a blanket over that piece of meat there.'

The man thus addressed hurried to Owen's body and draped a blanket over the ominously still form.

'Get that Swede out here.'

For a moment no one moved. Bassinet caressed the butt of the deadly Colt hanging at his hip. 'Funny the way a killing stirs the blood. I just might be tempted to take the odd shot at anyone as crosses me. Now, when I say, get that Swede out here, I mean, get that Swede out here.'

Bassinet glared coldly at a couple of Duke's men. They dropped their eyes, glanced at each other and then moved quickly into the cave. Moments later they reappeared supporting Owen's friend, Adam. His hands were bound and he was bleeding profusely. There was a dazed and confused look in his eyes.

Bassinet looked around and spotted an egg-shaped, upright boulder.

'Prop him against that there boulder.'

Adam was moaning with pain as the men pulled him across to the boulder. While this was going on Bassinet walked to one of the gunmen.

'Give me your gun belt.'

Without demur the man did as he was told. Bassinet walked to the big man leaning against the stone support. His guards were still standing each side of Adam waiting for further orders from Bassinet. He handed the borrowed gun belt to one of the guards.

'Strap that on him.'

The gunman watched as his orders were carried out.

'Swede, I'm giving you a chance. You snuck up behind me and beat me into the ground. Then you did an intolerable thing. You took my shooters and dunked them in a water-trough. No one hits me and lives to tell the tale. No one touches my pistols, and especially no one dunks them.'

126

The gunman glanced around at his audience as if to make sure they were appreciating his performance.

Celia, Rosalind and Henry huddled together. Spread around were the men who had ridden out to hunt for Duke's daughter. Isolated and apprehensive was Oliver Lismore. He made one last plea to the gunman.

'We ain't got time for all this, Josh. Let's ride in with the good news for Duke.'

'Watch and learn, Oliver. This is where one goddamn son of a bitch learns not to mess with Josh Bassinet.

'You listen up good, Swede. I'm giving you a chance to finish what you and me started that day back at Ayli. I could just shoot you down now like a dog. Or you can come quiet into Henderson and be hanged along with these other rustlers. You think you are mighty good with your fists. Well let's see how good you are with a gun. You see, a gun is a great leveller. It don't matter how big or how small a man is, with a gun in his hand he is equal to the next man. So I'm gonna walk back a piece and when you're ready we'll shoot it out. I'm gonna be fair with you. I'll let you draw first before I go for my iron.'

With that the gunman turned and walked back about twenty paces. When he turned his lips were drawn back in a feral grimace.

'Stop it!' Celia struggled as Howard held her from running forward.

Rosalind started forward but a brawny arm stopped her. She wanted to turn her head away but was unable. Along with the whole group of onlookers she felt compelled to watch the brutal scene being acted out before them. Bassinet held them all in fear like some dangerous reptile.

27

Owen felt that someone with the jagged top from a discarded bean can was using it to gouge a hole in the side of his head. Waves of pain radiated across the top of his skull. He opened his mouth to scream but discovered his mouth had been stuffed with cotton. In unbearable agony he unglued his eyelids.

Slowly he raised his head. A fire now started in his temple, adding new agony. He would have screamed but for the cotton inside his mouth that prevented him from operating his tongue and throat. Sounds began to filter through to his dulled senses.

Something covered his head preventing him seeing his surroundings. Fearful of making some sudden movement that would jar his pounding head and increase the agony, he inched his hand forward and drew back the rough material draped over him. Agonizingly slowly he raised his head an inch at a time and stared out through pain-dulled eyes. As he lay there recollection of recent events came in patchy flashes of memory.

Bassinet. He remembered jumping Bassinet. The gun had come out of the man's holster at bewildering speed. The gun-flash had blinded him. A terrible blow to his head – then nothing. Now he could see the man out there in front of him. As his senses recovered Owen took in the scene. As he watched he felt the anger grow in him. When Bassinet spoke Owen realized what was about to happen.

'No . . .' He tried to mouth the syllable but no sound emerged. He was not sure how he coped with the incessant, brutal throbbing in his head but somehow he managed to get on all fours. Waves of anguish coursed through his body. He lowered his head in an effort to ease the swarming dizziness and saw the flintlock.

The weapon lay invitingly close. He had been carrying it when he came back to the camp and found Oliver and Bassinet in charge.

The weapon had let him down twice. Once when he had tried to shoot Stone and again when he had tried to club Bassinet. He blinked at the tiny shutter in the stock. It had jolted open when he had dropped it. Revealed in the little cavity were the flints that gave the weapon its name. Dully he looked at the lock and the facts registered. The flint was missing. Somehow the flint had become dislodged while in Sam's possession. No wonder the rifle had not fired. It took time for these vital factors to register.

With trembling hands he reached out and gathered the weapon to him. Concentrating on the task in hand he also tried to listen in to the events taking place just in front of him. Somehow he screwed the tiny flint in position and checked it was loaded. Then he cocked the piece. When he finished that task he concentrated on getting to his feet. So absorbed were the spectators that no one noticed his slow steady shuffle as he approached nearer and nearer to the confrontation taking place before him.

Owen brought up the rifle. The stock nestled against his cheek. He brought the sights to bear on the leather-clad man waiting to kill his friend.

'That's enough, Bassinet,' he tried to say but only a hoarse croak emerged. Owen swallowed hard and tried again. At that moment Bassinet shouted at the Swede.

'Are you yellow, Swede? You can beat a man to death with your bare hands. But when it comes to a fair fight on equal terms you turn lily-livered.'

He turned to grin at Oliver when he saw the blood-soaked spectre aiming the flintlock. His eyes widened and he stayed motionless, his hands hovering over those deadly Colts.

'I'll kill you, Bassinet, if you don't do as I say.' This time the words came out as Owen intended. There was a convulsive movement as the assembly turned to look at the blood-splattered youth swaying unsteadily as he confronted the gunman.

Bassinet eyed Owen as a cat examines its next meal. 'You're as hard to kill as a goddamn packrat,' he surmised.

'Drop your gunbelt,' Owen croaked and in spite of his concentration the flintlock moved off-target.

Bassinet laughed.

Owen fought to concentrate. The long rifle in his hands was getting heavier as he swayed unsteadily, trying to keep the sights on Bassinet's chest. The gunman reached for his belt-buckle. And at the same time he went for his gun.

There was no question of his speed. His gun was clear and coming up even as Owen squeezed the trigger. The fierce recoil knocked Owen off his feet. It was this that saved him from taking another bullet. As he went down he wondered briefly where his own shot had gone.

'Josh, watch out behind!' Oliver jumped towards his friend and tried to push him aside as Adam fired his pistol. He grunted and staggered as he took the bullet meant for Bassinet. The gunman pivoted and his aim was true. His shot took Adam high in the chest. The impact threw the big man back against the rock. Even with a bullet in him the Swede raised his pistol and fired again.

Bassinet's pistols flared and bucked as he put bullet after bullet into the big man in front of him. While the shooting was going on Owen managed to get to his feet again. Like a drunken man he staggered towards the gunman.

The pain in his head was excruciating. Each time his foot connected with the ground a sharp explosion went off inside his skull. He saw Adam slide down the rock against which he had been propped. Even as he fell the big man was trying to bring up his pistol. Owen swung the flintlock at Bassinet.

The gunman was staring at Adam's dying efforts to bring his gun to bear. At the last moment saw the barrel of the flintlock swing towards him. Too late he tried to duck.

The heavy metal barrel thudded into his forehead. He staggered back. Owen swung again. This time the metal struck Bassinet above the ear. The gunman went down on one knee. In spite of the blow he was still trying to bring the six-gun to bear on his attacker. He never saw Rosalind behind him as she brought the fire-iron down on the back of his head. The gunman went down, the deadly Colt spilling from his hand.

Suddenly Celia and Henry were beside Owen as he swayed and almost toppled over onto the fallen gunman. Duke's men were crowding round also.

'Grab that son of a bitch,' someone growled as they surrounded Owen.

'Get back!' Rosalind was standing over Bassinet – the gunman's black Colt clutched in her hand. She swept it round at the crowd of men now menacing Owen. 'I'll shoot the man who touches any of my friends.'

The rush forward stopped and slowly the men backed away. The ragged youth looked capable of doing what he was threatening to do.

'The kid's right,' the big man, Howard, called. He

stepped up and stood facing his own men. 'There's been enough shooting.'

It was all that was needed. Grumbling and surly, the men backed down.

'Miss Celia, I came out here to find you and return you to your father.' Howard pointed to the bodies now littered around the rocky arena. 'This ain't what we came for. I reckon we'll take orders from you from now on in.'

Celia, still supporting Owen, nodded. 'Thanks, Howard, I guess you can take this fella,' she pointed to the unconscious gunman, 'and his companion back to town. Tell Father I shall be returning soon. I have some sorting out to do.'

Rosalind handed the Colt to the big man now offering to help Celia. He tucked the weapon in his waistband as he turned to his companions.

'You fellas, help Bassinet to his horse – Lismore too.' He was frowning as he looked at the men on the ground. A spreading red stain could be seen on Oliver's shirt. 'Goddamn! Lismore's been shot.'

Owen heard the observation. He stumbled over to his brother and dropped to his knees beside him. 'Oliver.' He looked with dismay at the blood on his brother's shirt.

Owen looked around. 'Help me,' he called. 'My brother's been shot.' He felt utterly helpless. 'Get them fellas that's inside the cave. Pete Thomson knows about wounds.'

Howard turned from supervising the exodus from the camp. 'Someone give me a hand to carry Lismore inside.' As the men moved to obey he looked critically at Owen. 'You look in a pretty bad way yourself, fella.'

'Damn how I feel! What about Adam?'

Howard reached out and laid a hand on Owen's shoulder. 'I'm sorry, fella. He didn't make it.'

Owen stared with disbelief at the big cowhand. He

turned and looked over towards the rock against which his friend had been leaning. Ominous stains showed up on the boulder. Beneath the rock huddled a dark shape.

'No . . .' he whispered.

Howard tried to restrain him. 'It ain't pretty, kid. Best you let him lie. When we get back to town I'll have a wagon sent out for your brother. We'll take your friend in at the same time. He'll get a decent burial.'

Pushing Howard aside Owen staggered towards the body. His throat choked up as he saw the ruined chest. A hand reached out and took his.

'I'm sorry, Owen.'

Looking up he saw it was Rosalind. He nodded dumbly, tears cascading down his cheeks and mingling with the blood of his dead buddy. 'He was my friend,' he mumbled. 'There is no one to take his place. Oh, Adam, why did you have to side with me?'

In spite of the gore Owen gathered Adam in his arms and hugged the bloody corpse. 'It's all my fault,' he moaned.

A comforting arm went round his shoulders. He laid his head against the girl's breast and sobbed as though he would never be able to stop.

'Come into the cave. When the time comes I'll help you with Adam.'

Owen allowed the girl to help him to his feet. Waves of dizziness swept over him. He was glad to lean on the ragged girl who had helped him take down Bassinet.

'You're all right, Rosalind,' he mumbled. 'You're all right.'

28

Marvin Pond was coming out of the cave as Owen and his companion approached. 'Owen, how are you?' Marvin peered closely at the blood-splattered youngster. 'Maybe there's no need to ask how you are. You look like you been wrestling with a mountain lion and come off second best.' He glanced at the dirty youth by Owen's side. 'Howdy.'

'Pa, is that you?'

Pond looked uncertainly at the boy. 'I'm sorry, son, but I ain't your pa.'

'Pa, it's me, Rosalind. I come looking for you.'

Pond peered closely at the speaker. 'Rosalind . . . my Rosalind was a girl. But dang me, if 'n you sure don't look like her.'

'Pa, it is me, Rosalind. I'm dressed up as a boy. We figured it would be safer.'

Uncertainly Marvin Pond reached out a hand. He cupped Rosalind's chin and stared intently at her. 'Rosalind,' he almost whispered. 'My very own Rosalind – can it be true?'

Beside her Owen's head was spinning. The effort of staying upright was proving almost too much for him. 'What about Oliver?' he croaked.

'How thoughtless of me, kid,' Pond said contritely. 'I'm afraid he's in a bad way.' He turned and motioned to one of the bunks. 'Pete and Celia have been tending to him. I have to warn you, kid, it doesn't look good.'

Owen moved forward and swayed dangerously as waves of dizziness threatened to overwhelm him. Rosalind was by his side immediately.

'Lean on me. I'll guide you across.'

Celia was just taking a blood-soaked wad from Oliver's chest as they approached. She smiled wanly at him. Pete Thomson handed her a clean pad. Gently she pressed it onto the crimson mess that was Oliver's chest. Owen stared at his brother. His face was grey and deep lines of pain had aged him considerably. Owen knelt beside Celia.

'Can I take over now?'

'Keep a gentle pressure on the pad.'

She turned away quickly and Owen did as she instructed. He saw her hands were stained red.

'Oliver, it's me, Owen. I'm sorry you were hurt.'

For a moment Owen thought his brother had not heard, then the eyelids slowly opened. 'Owen, how is Josh?'

'He's on his way back to Henderson.'

'Thank goodness for that at least. What a mess.'

The eyes closed and Owen thought Oliver was finished, but the lips moved again – the voice whispery and the words barely audible. 'You been a fool, Owen. You shouldn't have gone against Bassinet . . .' The voice tapered off as the breathing became shallower.

'Listen, Oliver, hang on in there. They sent for a wagon to take you into town. You'll be taken care of.'

'If the wagon comes it'll be to take me to Boot Hill. Don't leave me out here, Owen. Bury me beside Pa. I'd like that.'

Blood was trickling out of the side of Oliver's mouth. Owen stared helplessly at his brother. He knew that Oliver was right and that he was indeed dying.

'You can't die, Oliver. I got no one to take care of me.'

The eyes opened. 'You can take care of yourself, Owen. You're one selfish bastard. You proved that today. You're mule-headed just like Pa. I'm glad Josh is all right. You shouldn't have let Adam hit him that day. No one ever dared to do that to him before. He'll kill you for sure.'

Owen kept quiet not knowing how to reply.

'Bury me with Pa. When Josh catches up with you you'll be joining me.' Oliver's eyes were open but there was a terrible blankness in them. 'You still there?'

'Yeah, Oliver.'

'It's gone dark now. Maybe I should sleep . . .' But the eyes did not close and Owen knew his brother had slipped away.

'Sure, Oliver, you sleep now,' Owen whispered. There were no tears – only a deep void inside him as he stared at his brother's slack face. 'I'm sorry we never saw eye to eye. I'll watch over you. I'll stay here with you while you sleep.' He felt gentle hands on his shoulders and Rosalind's voice.

'I'm sorry, Owen. I'm so sorry,' she said.

He tried to stand but the effort was too much. His head was pounding and heavy. He rested his head on his brother and the darkness took away the sorrow and the pain.

When he opened his eyes he knew he was dreaming. The person he most hoped to see was there, watching over him. Her green eyes were studying his anxiously.

'Owen, thank goodness. We were worried about you. That head wound looked bad.'

'Pa always said us Lismores were a hardheaded lot. Said as we got it from Mother.' His head was throbbing with a dull soreness.

She reached out and gently stroked his cheek. In spite

136

of the pain in his head a warm glow coursed through his body. He was afraid to close his eyes in case it would end the dream. 'I never got to thank you for saving me from the sheriff.'

She smiled and he noticed the dark bruise on her cheek. 'I hit you in that cabin. I sure am sorry about that.'

She nodded. 'It's all right. I probably deserved it. I was trying to stick a knife in you.'

She kept her hand on his cheek. Slowly he reached up and laid his own large hand on hers. 'This is not a dream?' he asked seriously.

'No, Owen, this is not a dream.'

'How come you ended up in that hell hole of Eden?'

She told him everything then. How she and Celia had come in disguise in search of her father and how Jasper Stone had taken them prisoner.

'Then my hero came to the rescue. Thanks to you I've found my father.'

'I guess you're right.' The weariness suddenly overcame him and he slipped back into unconsciousness.

29

Her breasts were inches from his face and moved about disconcertingly. Owen had tried closing his eyes but a peculiar dizziness made his head swim and he had quickly opened them again. Next he had tried swivelling his eyeballs to the side but that only increased the throbbing in his head and made his eyes ache.

'Try and keep still, Owen. I'm no expert nurse and I want to get this bandage on right. I don't want it unwinding the first time you try to walk.'

Instead of speaking he tried to nod. He couldn't speak. His throat had dried up.

'Tsk! Are you even listening to me, Owen? I said, keep still.'

Rosalind stood before him winding a cotton bandage around his head. In order to get close to the task she had pushed her legs each side of his knee and was concentrating on keeping the bandage tidy and tight. Sheer will power kept him from groaning aloud.

Desperately he tried to think of something to distract him. His mind was blank or rather he wished it were blank. Instead it was filled with the curved, ample figure of the girl trying to bandage his wounded head.

He was seated on the bunk, his face level with her breasts. Those breasts seemed to have a life of their own and with every movement of her body they quivered enticingly just inches from his face. It was embarrassing, agonizing and exquisite.

'Is he being a good patient?' Pete Thompson loomed up beside Rosalind. 'You must have a head carved from Arden rock. I found a bump on top of your head as big as an egg and a bullet track down the side of your skull you could drive a herd of longhorns along.'

'Howdy, Owen.' Celia appeared beside them and linked her arm inside Pete's. She smiled sweetly up at the young rustler. 'Pete says you'll make a good recovery. A week or two in bed and a pretty nurse to attend to you is what he recommends.'

'He keeps wriggling around,' complained Rosalind. 'Anyway, I'm almost finished now.'

She leaned forward to tuck in the tail-end of the bandage and in doing so pressed her breasts firmly against Owen's face. He gulped and then succumbed to the agreeable, fresh smell coming off her young body.

'There now.'

The breasts moved back from his reddening face. He tried not to stare too obviously at them.

'It'll take a week or so before you are feeling fit again,' Pete said.

Just then Marvin Pond intruded on the little group. 'Howard has arrived with the wagon. He says he has to take Celia back to town otherwise her pa is forming a posse to raid up into these hills.'

Celia was biting at her lower lip as she turned to Pete. 'I'll have to go, Pete. I don't want to be responsible for any more bloodshed.'

'Miss Celia, I ain't been honest with you. I ain't what you think.'

Celia turned puzzled eyes to the speaker. 'What you saying, Pete?'

Slowly Pete reached inside his jacket. The little group were staring at the young man, wondering what was coming. Something metallic gleamed in his hand. Celia's eyes grew round with surprise.

'A badge – what does this mean?'

'It means I'm a law officer.' He sighed deeply. 'I been working under cover trying to find out what Leonard Duke was up to. You see, your father is wanted back in Billings for fraud and theft and, I'm sorry to say, murder. It took a long time to track him down.

'Owen's father, Alex Lismore, sent a wire to the marshal's office asking for information on Duke. Before we could act on the tip-off Alex Lismore was dead. We realized then the enquiry had to be under cover. I joined this band of rustlers when I found out that each man here was somehow a victim of Leonard Duke. If these men will agree to testify in a court of law there'll be enough evidence to convict.'

Celia was staring at Pete Thomson with a stricken look. Without a word she turned and ran from the cave. Pete stared after her. His face held the look of a dog that has just been kicked by his mistress. He looked at Rosalind.

'I didn't know she was the daughter of the man I had come to apprehend. When she first came in here we . . . we seemed to strike it off straight way. Goddamn it!' He turned his face away from the watchers.

Rosalind moved to his side. 'You really like her?' she asked softly.

Pete looked at her. He could not speak but nodded dumbly.

'She's a good person,' Rosalind said. 'She's not like her father. Far from it; she's good and decent and loyal to her friends. She would have known nothing about her father's activities. Since she met you she's mellowed considerably. I can't believe the change in her. She used to be so prickly.

Now she's as pleasant as a Sunday-school teacher. I guess all was lacking in her life was a good man to sweeten her up. You and she are good for each other. Let me go and speak to her.'

'Damn me, Pete Thomson, if you ain't the dark horse,' Marvin Pond exploded. 'Why the hell didn't you tell us you were a lawman?'

'I couldn't. I couldn't take the risk of it leaking out. I didn't want Duke to do what he has just attempted to do. I didn't want him to come out here and wipe out all my witnesses. I gotta keep you guys safe till I get you to court. Then Celia came along and I guess I fell for her. I reckon I messed that up too.'

Forlornly the lawman wandered to the mouth of the cave and stood there, a wretched, lonely figure outlined in the light from the outside.

'If that don't beat all,' murmured Tom Brennon. 'A dad-blasted lawman and he out there helping us rustle steers.'

'If you recollect he always was the one as stayed behind. I don't recollect him ever catching anything. Not like Bronco Kid here.' Pond turned to Owen. 'How are you, kid? My Rosalind taking care of you? She's been hovering over you like a mother-hen. Won't let anybody only herself look after you. Sat by your bed ever since you passed out on us.'

'I guess,' Owen said vaguely, not knowing how to respond to this information. 'What we going to do now? Celia will have to go back to town and face her pa. Sure puts Pete in an awkward situation. Seeing as how he's sweet on her.'

'I don't know, son.' Marvin Pond replied. 'While I been here hiding out from the law and Leonard Duke I did me a lot of thinking. Took to reading me some Shakespeare. One thing he did say that made sense. *All the world's a stage, and all the men and women merely players.* I guess that's true enough. We come on and play our parts and then we exit.'

Owen stared up at the older man. 'Is that all life is – just a show? I sure as hell don't like my part up till now. I've lost a good friend and a brother and father. Well, I'm gonna change all that. From now on I'm making my own action.'

Tom Brennon intervened, 'Look, kid, don't get into a discussion with that old cynic. He'll have you going out and blowing out your brains before you know it.' He reached forward and picked up a weapon familiar to Owen. 'Here you are, kid. I cleaned this piece up for you. It's a good tool. Thought you might like to have it as a keepsake.'

Owen looked at the flintlock. The stock was polished and the metal glowed with a brightness it never had when Sam owned it.

'Thanks Tom.' He was staring at the weapon with a strange light in his eyes. 'You know about guns?'

'Should do. It was my job to train the troops. Then got tired of giving guns to kids that went out and got their heads blowed off.'

'What sort of range is it accurate at?' An idea was growing in Owen's head.

'This is one of the later models with the rifled barrel. It'll kill at two or three hundred yards. You thinking of going hunting?'

Owen nodded slowly. 'There's a snake I'd like to get my sights on.'

Tom stared at him and then shook his head. 'It'll be a week or so before you are ready to go hunting snakes or any other kinda game. Maybe that head injury has mixed up your brain a mite. Talking to Marvin Pond don't help any, either. We got more important things to worry about than snakes, 'less they be human snakes.'

Owen hefted the weapon and walked outside. He felt light-headed with the effort of walking the short distance. The wagon was already loaded – the two tarpaulin-wrapped bodies lying in the back. Howard sat in the driver's seat with Celia sitting stiffly beside him. Pete was standing miserably watching the girl. She did not turn her head. Owen approached the wagon. Howard nodded to him.

'We're about ready to set out now.'

'Tell me about Bassinet.'

Howard tipped back his hat and stared down at the youngster. 'What you want to know?'

'Where's he hang out?'

'Spends most of the time down at the Lucky Star. He used to do that when he was with your brother in town. Ain't changed his habits since.'

Owen nodded. 'Thanks Howard, you been a square shooter in all this mess.'

The big man looked shrewdly down at the youth. 'You thinking of going up against Bassinet?'

'Got no choice. He killed my brother and my best friend.'

'I don't mean this in no way disrespectful, Owen, but you won't stand a cat in hell's chance against Bassinet. Ain't no one as fast as him.'

Owen nodded. 'I know. I seen him in action. Faster than a rattlesnake.'

'With the same nature too. Don't do it, kid. Ride away from it. Somewhere there's another gunman faster than Bassinet. He'll get his someday, with any luck sooner rather than later.'

'Do me a favour, Howard. Tell Bassinet I'm coming in. Tell him if he's still in town when I get there I'll kill him. After that I'll be able to bury my family in peace.'

Howard looked pityingly down at the youth. Perhaps he

143

was comparing this youngster standing before him with the pale, set face and bandaged head with the leather-garbed gunman he was contemplating going against. He shook his head resignedly. 'I'll tell him, kid. I see you're set on committing suicide.'

'Just you make sure Bassinet gets my warning.'

Howard flicked the reins and the wagon lurched forward carrying the remains of Owen's family into town to await their final resting-place.

30

Owen turned and saw Rosalind behind him. Before she could say anything Pete Thomson spoke.

'You serious about going after Bassinet?'

Owen was acutely aware of Rosalind nearby. Then Marvin Pond and his two companions were gathering round.

'You're crazy, kid. It's like Howard says, plain suicide.'

Owen looked steadily at the lawman. 'Bassinet killed my brother and my best friend. Sheriff Porter sure as hell will never arrest him for murder. It falls to me to bring him to justice. Besides, I'll never be able to rest easy while Bassinet lives. Someday he'll come after me. I don't want to live the rest of my life wondering when he'll come looking for me.'

Owen turned and walked past the little group, into the cave. When the others followed they found him strapping on the gunbelt Adam had given him on the night he went on the cattle raid.

'Owen, this is madness,' expostulated Marvin Pond. 'At least wait till you've regained your strength.'

Owen looked up at the little group of people gathered around him. He realized these were the only friends he had left in the world. 'It's been a real privilege to have known you. I'll never forget what you did for Adam and me when we first arrived here. When Duke is out of the way you'll be able to return to your homes. Then you'll all be welcome to visit me at Ayli.' He picked up his hat and gingerly placed it on his bandaged head. A figure stepped forward.

'Owen Lismore, you're not riding into town. We've just patched you up from one battle with that killer.'

Owen looked into the tear-filled eyes of Rosalind. Of all the things he was riding away from this was the one he regretted the most.

'I . . . I don't want to lose you, Owen . . .'

Owen blinked, not knowing what to say.

'I love you, Owen Lismore. I guess I loved you the first time I seen you in that boxing-tent.'

She moved close then. Owen stood captivated by the lovely vision before him as she wrapped her arms around his neck. Her closeness brought a familiar warmth to his body. Tentatively he reached up and touched her wet cheek. 'I guess I love you too, Rosalind.'

She kissed him then, long and lingeringly. When at last they stepped apart Owen felt the twin pangs of joy and sorrow lance through him.

'I have to go, Rosalind. Can't you see that?'

She did not reply. Tears were coursing down her cheeks and dripping unnoticed onto her shirt.

He picked up the flintlock and walked outside. As he saddled up he could see his friends in a huddle discussing something.

'Don't think of trying to stop me,' he called over. 'I got a plan.'

He swung into the saddle. The sudden movement sent a wave of dizziness through his injured head. He had to hold onto the pummel of the saddle for a few moments. When the world settled back on an even keel he tugged at the reins. His pony responded immediately and he rode out of the rustlers' camp without a backward glance.

*

As Owen neared town he looked for the gaudy tents down in South Meadows where he had first met Rosalind and her friend Celia. The place stood forlorn and empty. The show had moved on to another town. He had not pushed his mount, for his head wound throbbed painfully with every movement. Now he cantered slowly past the first buildings of the town. Across his saddle he held the flintlock. He had carefully loaded and primed it before entering town.

Businesses were winding down with the end of the day in sight. The saloons would be filling up. Owen knew where the Lucky Star was. As he approached the saloon he yelled out:

'Bassinet, I'm looking for you.'

The shouting elevated the throbbing in his head to a painful new level. He concentrated on the task in hand and allowed the pony to carry on down the street past the saloon.

'Bassinet, come out of whatever snake-hole you're hiding in. It's Owen Lismore. You murdered my brother.'

People in the street were turning to stare at the rider. Owen heard footsteps running but did not turn around. He knew if Bassinet had not heard his challenge then someone would surely run and tell him. He kept on riding.

More and more people were coming onto the sidewalks to witness this drama so unexpectedly taking place on their main street. The town hushed as the onlookers awaited the outcome. Some felt sorry for the youngster so evidently riding to his death. All knew Bassinet's reputation with a gun. No ragged youngster with a bandaged head and an old flintlock could hope to live long by foolishly calling out the top gunslinger.

147

'Bassinet, are you too yellow to come out and face me?'

The shot when it came was shockingly loud in the still evening. In spite of his resolve Owen flinched and a cold sweat added to his general discomfort. He pulled up his mount and slowly turned her around. At the other end of the street, dark and ominous, stood the black figure of death he had ridden in to encounter. In his hand the gunman held a smoking Colt. With a little flourish the gun was back in the holster.

'Here I am, Lismore,' he called. 'I'm glad you came by. I ain't killed nobody today.'

Owen slid from his pony. A slap on the rump sent it on its way. For a moment he swayed as a wave of dizziness swept over him, then by sheer will power he steadied. The rifle was gripped in his hands.

'I've come to finish this once and for all, Bassinet. Your killing days are done.'

'You want to be buried alongside your brother. I was thinking of taking over the Ayli when I've put you under. I think Oliver would have appreciated that.'

For a moment he was back at the Ayli and Adam was sparring with him.

'*Jus you listen to ol' Adam here. You gotta box. Don't mix it. Dat der John Charles knows a lotta dirty tricks when he git in close. He really hurt you if you let him get you in clinch. Keep you distance.*'

Bassinet started to walk down the street towards his opponent.

'Keep your distance,' Owen gritted.

Underneath the bandage his head was hurting bad. The ride into town had taken its toll on his resilience. He cocked the rifle, the click of the mechanism loud and clear in the quiet of a town holding its collective breath. He raised the weapon and rested the stock against his shoulder. He remembered the last time he had fired the piece at Bassinet and the recoil had thrown him backwards. And so he braced his feet.

'*Balance is everything, Owen. When you boxing place one foot behind the other. Dat way when you get hit you doan go down.*'

The oncoming gunman saw the movement and smoothly went into action. Almost without perceptible movement both guns appeared in his hands. The blast from the double shots stunned Owen's already stretched nerves. For a moment he wavered.

He could not tell if the bullets had come anywhere near him. But the distance for accurate shooting with a handgun was much too great. There was no indication that Bassinet's shots had come anywhere close. He gritted his teeth and centred the sights on the black-clad figure advancing inexorably towards him.

'*Keep you distance, Owen. Doan let him get close.*'

For a moment his sight blurred. He blinked rapidly. The sight on the end of the long barrel wandered. Owen held as steady as he was able. He concentrated on keeping the gunman in focus.

Bassinet continued walking and firing at the same time. Owen pulled the trigger. The rifle butt slammed into his shoulder. A puff of smoke blew into his eyes. The flash from the powder blinded him. Rapidly he blinked. Then, dropping the stock to the ground, he reached for the powder-horn. He knew he had to reload before Bassinet got any closer. His hand fumbled with the powder. The revolver shots had ceased.

He squinted his eyes and peered down the street expecting to see the gunman reloading his deadly Colts for another assault. A dark figure was sprawled in the dirt of the street. The arms were flung out each side. In the hands were gripped a pair of black Colts. There was no movement from the spread-out body.

Owen swayed unsteadily as reaction set in. Gritting his

teeth against the dizziness that was threatening to over-whelm him, slowly he began to pace forward. He was vaguely aware of the people on the sidewalk as he paced onwards.

'Goddamn see that. The kid took out Bassinet.'

'Never live to see the like of this again.'

'Blowed a hole in him big as a hat-box.'

The crowd were edging forward to see the fallen gunman. After seemingly walking for miles Owen came at last to the collapsed form. He looked down at the dead man. A gaping hole showed in the middle of the chest. Death must have been instant.

'He killed my brother and my best friend,' Owen said dully to no one in particular. 'I reckon the debt is paid in full. He'll murder no more.'

'Owen Lismore.' The voice cracked out loud and authoritative. 'You're under arrest.'

31

Owen looked up. Sheriff Porter was there. Beside him was a large man dressed in a business suit. With them were three men who were obviously of the same profession as the man he had just killed.

'Just lay that rifle down gentle and then hand over that six-gun I see you wearing. I don't want you killing any more citizens in this here town.'

Owen stared blankly at the men ranged before him. The only one he recognized was Sheriff Porter and that was because of the badge he was wearing on his vest. He guessed the man in the suit was Leonard Duke. Ignoring the sheriff's instructions he studied Duke. The man had a faint smile on his face as if he were enjoying the show. On either side of him ranged the gunmen – watching his every move – hands hovering over gun butts.

'Hi, Leonard, been a while ain't it.'

The voice came from behind Owen. He recognized Marvin Pond's voice.

Duke's face hardened. 'Pond! Well, well, we got them all now. A killer caught red-handed and a rustler. Sheriff!'

Sheriff Porter's face had gone pale. He was staring past Owen as if a ghost from his past had suddenly appeared.

'You ... you're under arrest, Pond,' he managed to stutter. 'Hand over your weapons and—'

'Hang on there, Sheriff,' an authoritative voice cut in from behind Owen. 'My name is Pete Thomson, US marshal. I got a warrant against Mr Duke for past crimes. I want you to put the handcuffs on him in order that I can escort him back to Billings to stand trial for fraud, extortion and murder.'

If anything, Sheriff Porter's face went even paler. He stared aghast at the men lining up behind Owen.

'Sheriff, these are all wanted men,' Leonard Duke snarled. 'They're a bunch of no-good rustlers. Do your duty and arrest them. Me and my men'll back you.'

As he spoke he stepped back a pace from the front line and swept back his coat. A holstered gun was exposed. On either side his men spread out slightly, watching with reptile-like eyes. These were deadly men used to fast action and killing. Leonard Duke paid well and these men were ready to do the job he paid them for.

'Sheriff Porter, I've deputized these fellas. You are up against an official posse. I must warn you that if you buck the Justice Department and take action against these men you are placing yourself outside your jurisdiction. Now what'll it be, Sheriff? You want to stay on the side of the law or you want to go on the run with a wanted on you?'

Owen was not looking at the sweating Sheriff Porter. Instead he was watching the tall, lean man with the drooping moustache. Instinctively he could see in him the same qualities of ruthless deadliness that Bassinet had exhibited.

The air was electric with tension. It was as if all motion around these men was suspended. For what seemed interminable moments nothing moved. Somewhere a horse flickered. Briefly Owen wondered if it was the cowpony he had ridden into town. He wondered also if Rosalind were somewhere watching all this.

Owen, I love you, she had said before planting a red-hot

152

kiss. His lips tingled at the memory. Then everything went into blurred motion.

Leonard Duke plucked his six-shooter from his holster. Owen heaved his antique rifle at the tall gunman and grabbed for his own six-shooter. Sheriff Porter threw himself to the ground and covered his head in his arms.

The gunman ducked as the rifle flew through the air aimed at his head. It slowed him down a fraction. Owen had no memory of how his own gun got into his hand. He was pumping shots at almost point-blank range at the men lined up before him. From behind him and from in front of him gunfire blasted out. All was smoke and thunderous noise and confusion. Then Owen was clicking on empty cartridges. The noise abated. Owen stared around, dazed and deafened.

Of the men who had lined up in front of him none was standing. Sheriff Porter still cowered on the floor. The gunmen who had flanked Leonard Duke were stretched out in the dust, dark-red stains showing the bullet hits. Leonard Duke was kneeling on the ground gripping a bloody shoulder – his empty gun lying on the ground before him.

Owen turned to glance behind him. The men who had backed him were still standing and like himself, looking slightly dazed by the sudden action. Miraculously none seemed harmed. Pete Thomson holstered his gun and stepped forward.

'Duke, it's all up now. Your gun-slicks are dead. It looks like your tame sheriff has messed his britches and you are looking at a long term in the state penitentiary or maybe a rope.'

Duke shot the lawman a look of pure hatred. 'You'll never get me to trial. I still got money and men in this town. I'm a man of influence.'

'Whatever. For now you're coming down to the jailhouse.' The marshal turned to the clustering onlookers. 'Someone fetch a doctor for Mr Duke. Tell him to come down to the sheriff's office.' He ran a practised eye over the sprawled bodies in the street. 'I reckon an undertaker is needed for these fellas.' Contemptuously he kicked Sheriff Porter. 'Come on, you bag of jelly, as soon as you help me put this man under lock and key you can go home and change your pants. But give me that badge first. You ain't fit to wear it.'

The sheriff moaned as he stood on shaky legs.

'On your feet, Duke, that busted arm won't stop you walking under your own steam.'

As Leonard Duke climbed painfully to his feet, a diminutive female walked forward. Pete Thomson froze. He had faced the gunmen without a tremor but now it was obvious he felt helpless in the face of this new adversary. He watched her, a distracted expression on his face.

'Celia,' he whispered.

And Duke, seeing him sidetracked, took advantage of the moment.

Owen saw the uninjured hand dip into the waistcoat pocket and reappear with the pocket gun. 'No,' he yelled but he was too late.

The little gun spat out its deadly missile. He heard Pete Thomson cry out and then as Duke fired again he was on him.

The man was big and burly and even with a wounded arm he was no mean fighter. Owen cannoned into the man and flung him off balance. They both went down with the gun trapped between the struggling men. Owen grappled desperately for the gun. He could feel the hard metallic shape with Duke's hand wrapped around it.

With one hand he tried to keep the muzzle pointed away from him. With his other fist he punched the wound in Duke's shoulder. The gun went off again – the sound muffled by the closeness of their bodies. Owen felt the man beneath him stiffen. A loud groan escaped from Leonard Duke. Owen punched again. But the fight seemed to have gone out of the man. He slumped limply to the ground.

Still holding onto the gun Owen slowly rolled away. The little pocket-gun came with him, released from Duke's suddenly slack hand. Owen rolled further, then pointed the small gun at its owner.

As he stared at the man he suddenly realized that Leonard Duke no longer posed a threat. The man who had probably been responsible for his father's death and indirectly for the death of his friend Adam and his brother lay staring blankly up into the darkening sky.

32

The bell tolled steadily, sending out its doleful message. The town was subdued. The sidewalks were thronged with people in their best attire. This was the very street that just a few days ago had been the setting for a theatre of death. The undertaker and his assistant had carted the bodies away from the bloody arena. Now this day was another day of drama. Today Oliver Lismore and his Swede cowhand would be laid to rest in the cemetery.

The town was crowded, for many families had come in from the surrounding districts. They came because of the Lismore name. Many had known Alex Lismore and respected his courage and integrity and his stand against the greed and avarice of Leonard Duke and his gang of gunmen. Attending the funeral of his son was a mark of respect for a fine man and a good neighbour. They came too out of curiosity, for they wanted to see the youngster who had stood up to the gunman, Josh Bassinet.

They waited and watched for the funeral procession to begin. There was a subdued chatter from the sidewalks and occasional chastising of children who were becoming bored and boisterous. Suddenly there was a hush.

Two beautiful matched black geldings came into view. Proudly they pulled the hearse, their black plumes and burnished harness adding to the solemnity of their office.

Beside the horses strode the black-garbed undertaker – his stovepipe hat making him tall and imposing. The spectators craned their heads to see better and stood on tiptoe. More than the spectacle of the hearse they yearned for a view of the mourners.

A collective sigh of recognition went up at the sight of the young man pacing steadily behind the hearse. His bandaged head marked him out as the main protagonist in the duel of death that had taken place that fateful night.

This was the youngster who had braced the famous gunslinger, Josh Bassinet, and put an end to the legend of the fast gun. This was the boy who had finally finished off Leonard Duke and lifted the yoke of fear and misery from Ayli Valley.

By his side walked an older man who had taken part in the shoot-out. Many knew him only as the infamous rustler, Marvin Pond. Behind them walked the other men who had taken part in that deadly showdown. Those townsfolk who knew their names quietly mouthed the knowledge to their neighbours.

The young handsome man with his arm in a sling was Pete Thomson, a lawman who had come to bring Leonard Duke to justice. He walked, quiet and dignified, no sign of his badge of office. By his side walked two other men from that famous incident. One was Tom Brennon, a big man who walked with easy grace and there was Jack Hallam, smaller and more compact than his companion. It was a day of solemnity and quiet stateliness.

That same afternoon another funeral took place. This time there were few mourners. Just a young girl dressed all in black looking small and lonely and flanked by two large men, like protecting angels.

Celia Duke stared with quiet sorrow as the coffin was

lowered into the deep grave. There were no tears – just a deep emptiness within which she felt nothing would ever fill. She took the handful of soil from the offered platter then sprinkled it into the open grave.

'Goodbye, Father, perhaps I could have been a better daughter.'

Escorted by her guardian angels she walked to the gate of the cemetery where a carriage waited to take her back to her home. A single male figure stood to one side of the gate. He carried his arm in a sling. The girl hesitated then walked steadily on. The man doffed his hat as she approached.

'Miss Duke, I'm sorry for what happened. I'm sorry for your loss.'

'Thank you,' she answered keeping her eyes lowered.

'I . . . if there's anything I can do . . . I mean . . . you just got to ask . . .'

For the first time she looked directly at him. Big tears trembled in her eyes and spilled. These were the first tears she had shed since she was a child. Instinctively the man stepped forward, his good arm outstretched. She allowed him to hold her slight, trembling body. They stood like that for a long time.

The guardian angels looked away then walked a few steps and stood by the carriage. They glanced at each other and gave small knowing smiles.

'Looks as if it's going to be a nice day after all, Howard.'

'I guess you could be right at that, Henry. I guess you could be right.'

The two men looked up as another carriage approached. Rosalind was driving with Owen as passenger.

'Owen, will you look at that, it's Pete and Celia.'

Owen smiled. 'Sure glad to see them two together.'

'Maybe we could have a double wedding,' Rosalind said wistfully.

'Double wedding – who else is getting married?' Owen asked naïvely.

Rosalind closed her eyes and said, 'Dear God, send me a husband with some savvy, for the one you picked for me may not have gumption enough to get me to the altar.'